MURDOCH
MYSTERIES
Under the Dragon's Tail

THE MURDOCH MYSTERIES

MURDOCH

MYSTERIES

Under the Dragon's Tail

MAUREEN JENNINGS

TITAN BOOKS

A Murdoch Mystery: Under the Dragon's Tail
Print edition ISBN: 9780857689887
E-book edition ISBN: 9780857689955

Published by Titan Books
A division of Titan Publishing Group Ltd
144 Southwark St, London SE1 0UP

First edition: February 2012
2 4 6 8 10 9 7 5 3 1

Maureen Jennings asserts the moral right to be identified as the author of this work.
© 1997, 2011 Maureen Jennings

Visit our website:
www.titanbooks.com

What did you think of this book? We love to hear from our readers. Please email us at: readerfeedback@titanemail.com, or write to us at the above address. To receive advance information, news, competitions, and exclusive offers online, please sign up for the Titan newsletter on our website: www.titanbooks.com

A CIP catalogue record for this title is available from the British Library.

Printed and bound in Great Britain by CPI Group Ltd.

For Iden, with gratitude forever
for his love and support

My father compounded with my mother under the Dragon's tail and my nativity was under Ursa Major, so that it follows I am rough and lecherous.

SHAKESPEARE, *KING LEAR*

PROLOGUE

February 1887

THE WOMAN HAD BEEN LABOURING SINCE THE PREVIOUS afternoon and now her time was close. At first, she'd cried out with each wave of pain and the cold night wind snatched the cries and swept them down the hill where they dispersed in the frozen fields. Now as dawn crept closer, she only moaned, exhausted by her travail.

Dolly Merishaw, the midwife, squatted down beside the narrow bed to examine her patient.

"It's time to bear down, madam. Hold onto this and pull as hard as you can. At the same time I want you to think of making your motion into the commode and push. That's it. Push. And again."

Suddenly, there was a rush of fluid and blood from the woman's womb and she shouted, pulling desperately on the towel which was tied to the bedpost. She was swept up in waves of such primitive power that she could not possibly resist. Her anus and privates bulged, she shrieked again, certain she was about to be torn asunder.

"The baby's crowning, we're almost done," said Dolly. Her words were soothing but her thoughts were steeped in malice. "I know what's going on, my fine lady. You're hoping it will die, then nobody'll ever know. But it's going to live, all right. And I know. I know all about your sin."

CHAPTER ONE

July 1895

SUNSHINE WAS STREAMING THROUGH THE KITCHEN window, making the flies sluggish as they crawled across the pine table. Irritably, Dolly Merishaw swatted a few of them, brushing the carcasses onto the floor. Even that slight effort caused a stabbing pain behind her eyes. She tried to wet her lips but her tongue was thick as cloth. She picked up the beer jug from the sideboard, but there were only dregs left and a bluebottle had drowned itself in the bottom.

She knew the two boys were out scavenging along the Don River and that Lily was delivering laundry to her customers on Gerrard Street, but she resented the fact they weren't here to look after her, to bring her a pot of tea the way she liked.

"Useless slags," she said out loud.

Not that she ever uttered a word of appreciation when her daughter waited on her. In Dolly's opinion, Lily had forfeited the right to thanks.

She pushed up the window sash and stuck her head out. The air was warm and soft, the sun caressing. Early July was the best time of the summer, before the August heat roasted the city like a cut of beef.

Even for Dolly, the sight of the trees dappling the street was appealing, and she leaned her arms on the windowsill for a moment. Two women bicyclists rode by, both of them sitting straight and rigid at the high handlebars. One was wearing knickerbockers and leggings, and Dolly noticed a passerby turn and glare. Many people were offended by these new bicycling outfits, Rational Dress, as they were called, but Dolly approved. She was happy to see women upset male tempers.

She retreated back to the kitchen, wondering if she was well enough to go out. She decided she was. She fancied some calf's liver for her breakfast, and Cosgrove's, the butcher, wasn't too far. And she could go to the Dominion Brewery on Queen Street. They sold stale beer at a cheap price.

Her felt slippers loose on her feet, she shuffled off to the parlour to get dressed. Ever since they had moved to Toronto, Dolly had been essentially living in this one room, as she was usually too full to climb the stairs to her bedroom. She slept on a Turkish couch, and Lily brought her meals on a tray. It was not uncommon for Dolly to throw the food at her daughter if she was displeased and Lily screamed back, raw, wordless cries. In the kitchen the boys listened, ears pricked, wary as fox kits.

It took Dolly almost an hour to make the journey, but when she returned to the house, neither her daughter nor her foster sons had returned.

"Where is the slut?"

She poured herself some of the flat, bitter ale and took a long swallow. Her parched throat was eased at once. She put the package of meat on the table and opened it up, smoothing out the newspaper that the butcher had used to wrap the liver. Her glance was idle at first, but suddenly she paused, bent closer, and squinted at a photograph on the inside page.

"My, my, look who it isn't."

A smear of blood partly obscured the picture but the caption confirmed her. She plopped the liver on the table and carefully tore the piece out of the newspaper. She read the notice again. What luck. Good for her, but bad for the other one. Clutching the strip of paper, she trotted off to the parlour, moving with more vigour than she had in a long time.

The room was hot and buzzed with flies feeding off the remains of last night's stew. The curtains were still closed but she didn't open them. She could see well enough and she wanted privacy. Beneath the window was her prized desk. She went over to it, pulling out a leather thong that hung around her neck. The key was never anywhere else, and it was warm and greasy from nestling between her breasts. She unlocked the desk, rolled back the top, and sat down. There wasn't much inside. A blotter, a tarnished silver inkwell and steel pen, a jar of her special herbs, the tin where she kept her money. Usually she enjoyed counting the coins and the bills, but today she shoved the tin aside and pulled open the drawer at the back of the desk. Reverently, she took out a vellum autograph album. One of her clients had left it behind years ago, and Dolly had appropriated it for use as her record book. The cover was soft and supple, royal blue with the word *Friends* embossed in gold letters. The paper was thick and creamy. She placed the piece of newspaper on the blotter, wiped her fingers on her skirt, and opened the album.

It didn't take her long to find the entry she wanted. In the eight years that had passed since then, her business had lessened considerably, and over the last three years there were no birth entries at all. Carefully, she tore out one of the unused pages and placed it on the blotter. She picked up the pen. The nib was crusty with dried ink but usable, and the inkwell hadn't dried out. She stroked, "Dear –" Bugger! There was a blob of ink on the paper. Perhaps she'd better practise first.

"I'm sure you remember the occasion of our first meeting."

The only way a person would forget that was if they was dead and she knew that wasn't the case.

"I have had some family troubles which has forced me into changing my name for reasons of privacy as I am sure you of all people can understand."

Even writing that down made Dolly flush with anger. She'd

been ruined through no fault of her own.

"I did as good by you as I could. Times are hard, my business has fallen off. A small gratuity would be kindly received. Or else…"

Or else what? She could go to the newspapers she supposed, but she had the uneasy suspicion the owner would throw her out on her arse in short order. No, a word in the right places was better. Or rather, the threat of a word in certain ears. Dolly studied her note. That would do. She tore out another blank page and started to copy what she had written.

Lily lifted her face towards the puff of cool, evening breeze that came through the open window. She had almost finished her ironing, and her wrist and forearm were aching. The smooth, fresh linens were piled on the chair beside her. Dolly was sitting in the reed rocker by the window. She had consumed two large jugs of hard beer by now, and she was full. She had the album in her lap, but her brief good humour of the afternoon had vanished. As she rocked herself back and forth, she was muttering under her breath. "Stupid cow, they was all the same. Listened to some glib-glab from any man who wanted to stop his beak. Then when they had a natural in the oven they wanted Dolly to help. And she did. She was the best. But she was brought down. No fault of hers."

Lily, who was stone deaf, eyed her mother nervously, reading the signs the way a wild creature does and knows from the wind and the smell in the air that a storm is coming. The two boys were at the table. The younger boy, Freddie, had found a little lead horse in the mud of the river and he'd harnessed it to an empty matchbox. He was trotting it around the table, over the hedge of the plates, through the stream of the sticky spilled beer. George, bored and restless, was watching him. Then suddenly, he winked and reached in the basket for one of Lily's clothes pegs. He held it upright in front of the horse and carriage and motioned Freddie to give him the toy. With one savage rush, he smashed the peg flat and made the horse trample over it.

Freddie glanced over to Dolly in alarm, afraid she would see. He knew without ever saying so that George was exacting retribution on their foster mother.

"Pray for us now and in the hour of our death, Amen."

William Murdoch had said four Hail Marys and the Lord's Prayer three times, once in Latin. This was not because he was especially pious – he wasn't anymore – but because he had insomnia and repeating the familiar words sometimes lulled him to sleep. Not tonight. It was like trying to catch a fish with your bare hands. The worst thing was that tomorrow he had to get up at half past five to do his training ride. However, he'd heard the church on Queen Street toll out ten o'clock, then eleven, and shortly it would be dolefully chiming out midnight. Maybe he should reset his alarm clock and get an extra hour. He flung himself onto his back. Better not. The police athletic tournament was only four weeks away and he had to train hard if he was going to outride Varley, the new crack from number-three station. And beat the shicey bastard he would, or die in the attempt.

Bong, bong, bong.

Twelve midnight. He thought the bell ringer was hurrying it, keen to get to his bed probably. Where he would no doubt immediately fall into a blameless sleep.

From the parlour below Murdoch heard Arthur Kitchen, his landlord, coughing his perpetual, spongy cough.

His own body tightened up in empathy with the sick man. In spite of Beatrice Kitchen's best efforts the consumption was continuing its inexorable march, and Murdoch was afraid Arthur mightn't last out the year. All of a sudden his bed felt lumpy, and he turned over again trying to find a comfortable spot. Trying to get away from his thoughts. This next Christmas would be the second one without Elizabeth. If she had lived they might have had a child by now, the start of the family he yearned for. However, typhoid was no respecter of dreams and had ignored the desperate novenas he made when she fell ill, the masses he bought. "God took her to his bosom. He needed her more than you did," said the priest, and Murdoch, in a surge of blasphemous rage, barely held back from punching him in his prissy mouth. He, himself, was lucky to be spared, said the doctor, but he didn't feel lucky. For many months he had wanted to be dead too.

Bong, bong...

The last toll faded. He flopped his leg to the edge of the bed.

He and Liza had never had conjugal relations, of course. Once when they were alone in her sitting room, hot with desire, he had touched her breast. Because of her stiff corset, the gesture was as unsatisfying as stroking the armchair. She had laughed mischievously into his eyes. "Soon, Will, soon." But hardly one month later the fever swept the house where she boarded, taking off all of them and several more who'd been in contact with the place.

Murdoch thrashed in earnest. He knew when his mind went in this direction sleep was out of the question. Shut it off, he said to himself, but he couldn't. He'd never even seen her unclothed but he imagined her lying beside him, warm and soft.

When he was a young man working at the lumber camp near Huntsville, he'd got up his courage and asked one of the older men what connection with a woman was like. The logger, who spoke tenderly of his absent wife, contemplated his question for a moment, then said seriously, "It's a bit difficult to put into words, Will. The closest I can come is this. Imagine thrusting your member into warm mash, at the same time as you jump out of a tree."

Murdoch sighed again.

Annie Brogan pulled her garters over her silk stockings and shook out her skirt. She was wearing her stage clothes, a stiff taffeta dress of bold red stripes with an uncomfortably tight bodice cut low. She thrust her sore feet into her boots, wet the tip of her finger, and rubbed at the scuff marks on the toe. Part of her act was to dance with men from the audience, and some squab was always treading on her. She yawned and stared down at the man on the bed. He was naked, his now flaccid John Thomas draped limply on his fat leg. He snored and the thick nose-sound sickened her. In daylight with his nobby clothes on, she liked him well enough. He was generous. But always when he was like this, replete with his long-drawn-out screw, she felt such revulsion her own thoughts frightened her.

She yawned again, uncontrollably. She would have liked to sleep the night in that comfortable, clean bed but she knew Richard wouldn't want that. He preferred her to come and go unseen. The Yeoman Club where they had their rendezvous was convenient for that reason. Situated on River Street, it was a favourite place of well-to-do men who wanted luxury and discretion rather than a fashionable address.

The wick in the oil lamp was low, but she could see the money he'd left on the bedside table. She picked up the bills and tucked them into her finger purse. He always said it was for cab fare and she maintained the pretence. To think more deeply was unbearable. As she finished dressing, the brass clock on the mantel chimed the quarter hour. She almost giggled. Poor little Cinders, leaving the prince before her clothes turned to rags again.

This was a plainly furnished room, too sober for her taste, but she knew the members who used it weren't particular about the appearance as long as it cost dear. There was a pull-down bed, comfortable brown suede chairs, a fine glass cabinet filled with books, rarely opened. But best of all, the room had access to a private laneway.

She pulled aside the green felt curtain that masked the outside door. For a moment, she hesitated. She was not looking forward to what she had to do. Truth was she would have given anything not to go there. Not to see the woman again.

The night air was sweet-smelling, cool on her face. She closed the door softly behind her and stepped into the welcoming darkness.

CHAPTER TWO

MURDOCH ANTICIPATED THE BAWLING OF THE ALARM BY a fraction of a second and sat up immediately to switch off the bell. He peered blearily at the clock, then dropped back to his pillow to catch one more sip of shut-eye. As he lay, he heard a faint squeak of bedsprings from the adjoining room. The walls were thin and he hoped he hadn't disturbed Enid, his fellow lodger. He held his breath, listening, but there was no further sound. Sometimes he heard her whimpering in her sleep, making him ache to go and comfort her, but this morning both she and her boy were quiet.

He sat up, swung his legs out of the bed, and pulled off his nightshirt. He was ashamed at how persistently and vividly his imagination conjured up an image of the young widow sleeping curled up in her bed. He felt disloyal to Liza's memory.

He dressed hurriedly. His black woollen bicycle sweater was getting quite rank with sweat, but it would have to do until washday. Boots in hand, he tiptoed down the landing, using the light from his bicycle lamp to guide him. The house was silent; even Arthur seemed to have gained some peace. Before he became ill, he had been a crack wheeler and over the past few weeks they'd spent enjoyable evenings planning strategies for the upcoming race. At the last tournament, Murdoch had won the mile sprint, but this year he'd wanted more challenge and he'd entered the five-mile handicap. Tired and gritty-eyed, he berated himself as a flagellating fool.

Don't think, just keep moving. It'll be a chop when you get started. At this time of day, the air of the city was fresh, the streets clean. With all the sluggards still wallowing in sleep, he could ride on the sidewalks and avoid the horse droppings and dust of the road.

He crept down the stairs to the front hall where he stowed his wheel. He'd saved for a year to buy it – sixty dollars, almost a month's wages. The light from his kerosene lamp gleamed on the polished ram's horn handlebars. The finish was a modern maroon and the double tyres the best Morgan and Wright made. The bicycle was still new enough for him to experience sinful pride in the treasures of the world. A considerable amount of pride if the truth be known.

He manoeuvred carefully through the front door. Outside,

the dreaming street was hazy in the grey light of dawn. Suddenly, a cat yowled. Its rival answered and they both dashed across the road in front of him. The leading cat was black and thin, the other animal, a big marmalade, looked better nourished. Murdoch watched them disappear into the shrubbery of his neighbour's front yard. *The eternal conflict*, he thought, then grinned to himself. Liza had often chided him about finding allegories everywhere he looked.

He tugged his cap tight on his brow, mounted his wheel, and pushed off from the curb.

"Hear me, Varley, I intend to be the cock of this race."

George Tucker opened his eyes. As usual, his nightshirt was drenched in sweat. He always blamed their small, stuffy room, which retained the heat better than the Gurney did. In fact, he sweated nightly from a terror his survival depended on denying. He sniffed. There was a bad pong. Freddie had wet the bed as he always did when he was afraid. He'd moved as far to the edge as he could but George could feel the heat from his body, smell the stink of the other boy's breath. Viciously, he kicked out with his heel, connecting with a crack on Freddie's shin bone. With a cry the boy awoke and clutched his leg.

"You pissed again," said George, and Freddie's hands flew to protect his privates, where retribution was usually exacted. He didn't say a word, knowing from long experience it would do no good and was more likely to worsen George's ire.

"Get up, you stinking darkie face. It's late. She'll have our arses on a bandbox."

He sat up and scratched at his ankle, where a rash of new bites had come up in the night. It was impossible to eliminate the voracious bedbugs in the old house, and with the heat they flourished.

"I don't hear nobody," said Freddie.

George felt like kicking him again. He always did when the boy spoke so timidly. But he was right. Lily's bedroom was directly across from them but he couldn't hear her. When she washed herself in the morning she made strange humming noises, tuneless sounds, the way an old deaf dog might still bark at silent shadows. Not that Lily was old yet. Not young either but still with firm diddies and a round arse. George was considering trying out his sugar stick on her. Although nobody celebrated, he'd claimed July the thirtieth for his birthday and he thought this might be a present to himself.

"Where's Mrs. Mother?" asked Fred, who was sitting up in bed but waiting for George to move first.

George listened. The parlour was directly beneath them and they could usually hear Dolly moaning in her sleep, shouting at a bad dream, breaking wind noisily. She was always in a bad skin when she first got up and they were careful to stay out of her way.

"D'you think Lily's gonna get it?" asked Freddie.

"'Course she is."

In spite of his scoffing tone, George felt a pang of fear. The punishments that Dolly exacted on her daughter were fearsome to behold.

He got out of bed and went over to the slop pail to pee. Then he splashed tepid water on his face from the tin bowl on the washstand and pulled off his grubby nightshirt. Last week, Lily had washed his one shirt, a brown holland. He'd sat bare-chested until it was ready, arms hugging his bony ribs. George was ashamed of his size and yearned for the day he would grow taller and heavier. He slipped the shirt over his head. It smelled of carbolic soap and sunlight, a smell he liked. His plaid woollen trousers, however, were filthy, torn at the knee and too big. He'd acquired them last year on one of his hunts along the riverbank. Didn't matter that the owner was in swimming. George just walked away with the trousers over his arm, casually and calmly.

Underneath the clothes, his body was dirty and smelly but he didn't care. He never went to school, never associated with anybody who was clean enough to notice the difference. As long as he could remember he had lived with Dolly, although she was not his mother and never ceased to remind him of the fact. His own mother was a tart, a doxie who had kissed the devil's behind, which was why he looked the way he did and why she had abandoned him to Dolly's care when he was an infant.

"If it wasn't for me you'd have ended up in a pauper's orphanage," she said, and George often thought his life might have been better if he had.

"Get a move on," he said to Fred, who was watching him with dark, nervous eyes. Their first job was to scavenge along the river, then go down to the lakeshore. They searched mostly for firewood to keep the stove going, but they could expect a cuff from Dolly if they didn't come back with something she could use or pawn. She'd actually smiled at him once when he found a woman's earbob of silver filigree buried in the sand.

He listened again but there was no sound at all from the room below. He couldn't let go of the tight knot of fear in his stomach. They were all going to get it as soon as she woke up, not just Lily. And he knew for sure it would be bad.

CHAPTER THREE

MURDOCH, THINKING WEIGHTY AND MELANCHOLY thoughts about the capriciousness of life, watched two flies crawl around the lip of the saucer. One succumbed to temptation and fell into a sweet, sticky death, the other flew away. Because the stables were adjacent to the police station, it was impossible to keep the fly population anywhere close to bearable. However, Mrs. Kitchen had assured him the best way to catch flies was with a mixture of egg yolk and molasses and he'd placed two full saucers on his desk. So far he'd only netted four carcasses. It was more efficient to swat them. He dispatched two in quick succession, both unfortunately crawling across the portrait of Her Majesty which hung behind him and which was now pocked with tiny bloodstains. The matching portrait of Chief Constable Grasett was even more defaced but that was probably because Murdoch pursued the flies on that picture with more vigour.

He stretched his arms above his head and rubbed hard on his brow to wake himself up. He would have given a day's wage for a short kip, but he knew that if Inspector Brackenreid found him asleep it would be truly costly. The problem wasn't only his sleepless night. The cubicle that passed as his office had only one small, high window that let in plenty of flies and dust but not much air or light.

Yet another yawn rippled up his throat. The morning had been quiet and the only report he'd had to do was complete. A cabbie was charged with galloping his horse along Queen Street. He said he hadn't, that the horse had got the bit between his teeth, but two witnesses swore they'd heard him crack his whip. The case would go before the courts.

There was a tap on the wall outside the cubicle. Because the space was so small he'd done without a door and the entrance was hung with a reed curtain. He could see the outline of Constable George Crabtree looming on the other side.

"Yes?"

Crabtree pushed aside the clacking strips.

"There are two ragamuffins out front, sir, with some story about their mother being dead. They can't rouse her, they say."

"Dead drunk?"

"It's possible, sir, but they do seem quite ascared. Say she's gone stiff."

Murdoch stood up, welcoming the diversion.

Number-four police station was not the largest or busiest in the city but it maintained law and order over a diversified area. To the west and north were gracious homes on wide, tree-lined streets such as Church and Gerrard. To the east and south were run-down row houses, workmen's cottages, small businesses, and manufacturers' properties. Most of the crimes that elicited charges were for petty theft or drunk and disorderly conduct. Without exception these misdemeanours occurred in the east side.

Murdoch followed Crabtree to the main hall of the station. A high counter divided the room in half, on one side the upholders of the law, on the other their uneasy charges. Two boys were sitting close together on the wooden bench that ran around the far side of the room. They were barefoot and dirty.

"Hello, young masters, what's the problem?" Murdoch asked.

"She's dead, sir, stone dead." The older boy who spoke was scrawny, smelly, and ill-dressed. His eyes were badly crossed and this inability to meet a direct gaze made him seem shifty. His words tumbled out. "She didn't get up in the morning, see. No sign of her. I thought she might just be feeling under the weather so I took her in some tea. There she was on the floor, stiff as a poker."

"Hold on. Who're you talking about? Who's dead?"

"Our mother, Mrs. Dolly Shaw. You'd better come see, sir."

"Where is she?"

"In the parlour. She's stiff as a board," he said again.

"Your mother, you say?"

"She's not really our mother, I mean not blood, but we've always bin with her, haven't we, Freddie?"

He nudged his companion, who nodded vigorously. This boy was a quadroon, with dusky skin and light brown curly hair, very tangled. He kept his eyes to the ground except for quick anxious glances at his companion.

"And what's your relationship to each other?"

The older one looked puzzled. "I dunno, sir. I suppose we're brothers."

Murdoch didn't think that was biologically possible given how different they looked, but he didn't comment. He took out his notebook and pencil from his pocket.

"We'll come take a look. Where do you live?"

"Over on River Street, corner of Wilton. Number one-thirty-one."

"Your names?"

"I'm George Tucker, this is Alfred Locke."

Murdoch squatted down in front of the quadroon boy.

"Cat got your tongue, Alfred?"

He shook his head, shrinking back into the bench.

Murdoch straightened up.

"Let's go and see what's up, Crabtree."

"Shall I fetch the coroner, sir?"

"Not yet. We'd better find out what's happened first. I'll ride on ahead on my wheel. You bring the boys."

"Please, sir, can we come with you? We can run real fast, can't we, Freddie?"

Murdoch gazed at their worried faces and relented.

"All right. Come on. But I warn you I'm a scorcher."

They both smiled a bit.

In spite of what the boy had said, Murdoch had doubts that the woman was really dead. More likely passed out from too much jackey.

Annie could hear her sister moving about in the next room and she opened her eyes reluctantly. Sleep was a warm cocoon she wanted to stay in, and as consciousness returned the memory of the previous night inched closer like a poisonous spider that had been waiting for her to move.

She sat up, squinting her eyes against the bright sun trying to squeeze around the edges of the old velvet curtains at the window. There was a band of dull pain pressing behind her eyes.

"Mildred? Millie? What are you doing?"

Her sister answered from the kitchen. "I'm making tea."

"Good. I could do with that."

"There isn't enough for two."

Selfish tit, thought Annie.

"I don't mind if it's weak. Add more water."

Tentatively she swung her legs out of bed and waited, testing the level of pain in her head. A whet would be far better than a spot of cat-pee tea but there wasn't any. She had finished the bottle last night when she got home. She'd sat in the dark kitchen while Millie snored softly in the bed. She would have drunk herself into oblivion if there'd been enough gin but there wasn't.

Moving slowly, she pulled the chamber pot out from under the bed and squatted. Millie came in carrying a tin tray. She didn't look at Annie but plunked the tray on top of the washstand, pushing aside her sister's stays, which were draped there.

"Tea's finished, so's the bread."

"Can't you –"

"No. There's no more tick."

Her face was sullen and Annie could feel her own anger rising. Ungrateful bint. She got up from the pot and Millie handed her one of the cracked cups, took the other, and sat on the one chair by the bed. Annie inspected her cup, half filled with insipid tea, held it in both hands, and took a cautious sip.

"Ugh, what'd you do, wave a tea leaf at it?"

"Don't drink it if you don't like it."

"What's up with you?"

"It'd be nice for once to have a bit of money. You took all of it."

"Sod it, Millie, I had to pay for the medicine, didn't I?"

"What medicine?"

"What medicine? My ear lugs must be plugged up."

She put down her cup, and opened the drawer of the washstand.

"Here." She thrust a brown paper bag at Millie.

Reluctantly Millie opened it.

"What is it?"

"Those are special herbs."

"Where from?"

"A woman of my acquaintance."

"How d'you know they'll work?"

"They will, believe me."

For the first time, Millie looked directly at her sister, caught by her tone.

Annie shrugged. "Never mind that now. Come on. No sense in dawdling. You have to stew the whole lot in boiling water for half an hour, then you drink two cups every two hours until – well, until it works."

Millie put the bag on the washstand and averted her head.

"I'm not going to do it."

"What do you mean, 'I'm not going to do it.' Do we have a choice, my lady?"

Her sister began to weep, sniffy infuriating cries.

"I want to keep the baby."

"Then what? You've already bin warned. One more day off and you'll get canned."

"I was sick. I couldn't help it."

"And when the kid's sick and can't help it, do you think the boss'll understand? Bloody hell, Millie, you're a nickel girl, if that. They won't hold no job for you. And don't think you can count on me to watch the squawler."

"Don't worry, I wouldn't consider it."

"What then?"

Millie swallowed hard.

"I could put it up for adoption. There are lots of decent

people who haven't been able to have a baby of their own. Rich people."

Annie slapped her hard across the face and Millie screamed out.

"What's that for?"

"To wake you up, you stupid tart. It's easy to say that now when the thing is just gas in your stomach. Wait until it grows and moves and then comes out, a sodding flesh-and-blood baby. See if you want to let it go then. You might as well try to cut off your arm or your leg and give that away."

"Annie!"

"I never thought you'd be this stupid, Millie." She grabbed up the brown bag. "Here. Go and make the brew. I'll stay with you while you go through it even if I have to cut work."

Millie was sobbing in earnest. "I can't… it's him inside me, Annie. I'm carrying John. I can't get rid of his baby."

Annie grabbed her sister by the arms, and started to shake her.

"You nocky bint. Do you think he cared a piss where he dipped his beak? Do you? Answer me. I want an answer, you mardy tit. Do you think he cared which doodle sack he put it in? Carrying John my arse. He's bunked off, hasn't he? Like they all do."

Mildred's hair was coming loose with the violence of the shaking, and although she didn't fight back she was shocked into some semblance of backbone.

"He might be ill. That might be why he hasn't come to church. You don't know, Annie. You think you know everything but you don't."

Annie let her go in disgust.

"I know he's like any other flash man, lots of glib-glab, pushing to have a bit, and before you know there's a bun in the basket and no husband to be seen."

"He loves me, Annie, I know he does."

"Good. Good. If that's the case he'll marry you, won't he?"

Millie shook her head. "I told you it's not possible. He'll lose his job. His employer is very strict."

"You're a little liar, Millie Brogan. That's not the only reason. He can get another job. What is it? Is the sly arse married already?"

"No!"

"What then?"

"I can't say, you'll think the worst."

Annie raised her hand. "Tell me!"

"He's betrothed."

Annie snorted. "Ha. Well that's one engagement that's meant to be broken." She pulled off her nightgown and reached for her stays. "Come on."

"Where?"

"We're going to have a chat with John – what's the sod's name again?"

"Meredith."

"Merry Dick?"

"Annie!"

"Where does Mr. Merry Dick live?"

"Annie, we can't go there."

"We can and we will."

Millie lowered her head stubbornly but Annie yanked her hard by the hair, forcing her to look up.

"Would you rather I have a whisper in Reverend Jeffery's hairy ear? What would your good friends think about that?"

Her sister flinched, then said, "He's in service but I'm not sure where – a big house on Jarvis Street. He showed me once after church."

"Too bad it wasn't the only thing he showed you."

She let her go, then picked up the corset.

"Here, help me with this."

She held her breath while her sister laced her up.

"Give me my hairbrush."

Millie opened the drawer of the washstand and scrabbled through the jammed contents.

"It isn't here."

She started to look in the cupboard below, but Annie called out.

"Stop! It's not in there."

However, Millie saw the album that was stuffed at the back of the washstand. It was a deep blue colour with gilt letters that spelled *Friends*. Before Annie could prevent her she took it out.

"What's this?"

Annie snatched it away.

"Never mind. It's mine."

"Where did you get it?"

"I said never mind." She thrust it under her pillow. "Now come on. Find that brush else I'll do something to make you hurry."

Millie swallowed a sob. "Sometimes I think you hate me."

Once again, Annie caught her sister by the arms and gave her a shake but this time she was softer. "Silly bint. Of course I don't. I'm your sister, aren't I? Haven't I always looked out for you?" She gave her a kiss on the mouth. "Get yourself fixed up, little Sissie, we're going to pay a call on Mr. John Merry Dick."

With the two boys running beside him as fast as they could, Murdoch pedalled along Wilton towards River Street, which was only three blocks away. At the corner a small crowd of the curious had already gathered. George pointed to the house on the northwest corner, a dilapidated dwelling badly in need of paint.

"That's us," he panted. The short run had left both boys gasping.

Murdoch dismounted and, blowing his claghorn, pushed his bicycle through the edge of the crowd.

"Police! Make way! Come on, let me through."

The onlookers parted willingly, calling out to him.

"What's up, mister, what's happening?"

Eager faces gaped at him. It seemed he wasn't the only one whose morning had been dull.

"I'll be sworn if you want, sir," cried out one of the men.

Murdoch nodded in acknowledgement and opened the rusty gate in the iron railing that ran around the house. George and Freddie were close on his heels and he beckoned to the older boy.

"Hold my wheel. Don't let anybody touch it on pain of death."

"Yes, sir," said George and he looked proud. Freddie stayed right beside him.

A woman was sitting on the steps, her face buried in her apron. She was rocking back and forth, making strange keening sounds. A thin, grey-haired man was standing beside her, his hand on her shoulder.

"That's our Lily," called George. "She's the missus's daughter. She's a dummy."

Murdoch walked closer and the grey-haired man greeted him with relief.

"I'm Clarence Daly, a neighbour." He waved vaguely in the direction of one of the houses. "Lily here just clapped eyes on her mother." He patted her shoulder, kindly. "She don't hear nothing or talk much so I can't explain to her."

"I'm Acting Detective Murdoch. Where's the woman in question?"

"I'll show you," said Daly.

At that moment the crowd stirred again as Constable Crabtree, slightly red and sweaty from his fast jog to the scene, pushed his way to the gate. Murdoch was wearing his everyday clothes, fedora, brown tweed jacket and trousers. The woman on the steps had hardly seemed to pay him any attention. Crabtree, however, was in his navy-blue police uniform. He was a formidable man, easily six foot three, and his high rounded helmet added another good eight inches. The woman looked up and saw him come through the gate. She gave a high-pitched cry, an almost dog-like yelp, and scrambled to her feet. Before anyone could divine her intention, she jumped down from the steps and bolted along the side of the house. Immediately, Murdoch leaped after her and caught her as she tried to climb over the fence. He managed to grab hold of her arm but she screamed such a dreadful cry that he momentarily loosened his grip. She wrenched herself free and shoved him violently away. Off balance, he fell backwards on the ground, sprawling awkwardly. The woman half rolled, half vaulted over the low railing and ran off at full speed, disappearing almost at once into a laneway. A couple of boys started off in pursuit, but their mother yelled to them and they stopped like hungry hounds thwarted in the chase. The onlookers all stirred excitedly but nobody else followed the woman. Crabtree came over to Murdoch, who was scrambling to his feet, a touch embarrassed by his ungraceful fall.

"Shall I go after her?" the constable asked.

"Not now," said Murdoch, brushing dust from his trousers. "Let's go inside."

Daly hovered at the top of the steps.

"She's a high-strung girl that one," he said to Murdoch, like a host apologizing for a misbehaving child. He ushered them into the hallway. Uncarpeted stairs were directly ahead. To the left was a door hung with ornate burgundy portieres.

"In there," said Daly.

Murdoch pushed aside the curtains and entered the parlour. The room was small, hot, and dark. The stench was overpowering and there was the heavy drone of sated flies. He waited a moment to let his eyes get accustomed to the gloom. The body of a woman was lying on her back close to the hearth, her head resting on the brass fender.

He turned to the man hovering behind him in the doorway. "Mr. Daly, I'd thank you to stand outside for the moment."

"Right, sir." He happily obeyed.

Murdoch went over to fireplace, negotiating his way through the furniture that crammed the room. It was obvious the woman had been dead for several hours. Flies were crawling over her face, in her eyes and open mouth. Her skin was grey. Gently, he tried to move the chin. It was stiff, the rigor of death firmly established. He called to the constable, who had stayed in the hall.

"Crabtree, come in here, would you?"

The constable entered, grimacing as the odour hit his nose. Death had loosened the woman's bowels.

"Help me turn her."

Together they rolled the rigid body on its side. The post mortem staining in both of her hands and fingers was clearly visible. Black felt slippers were half on, half off her feet and in the bare heels was the same purple coloration. She had died in the position they found her. She was wearing a grey flannel dressing robe and an old-fashioned white mobcap. A few strands of hair of an unnatural auburn tint had escaped and draggled about her face, looking like rivulets of bloody tears.

"Hold her up for a minute, will you, Crabtree?"

Near the base of the skull, the cap was marked with a rust-coloured stain. Gingerly, Murdoch lifted up the edge. The hair was matted underneath with what he assumed was blood.

"Hard bash to the noggin by the look of it."

Crabtree grunted. "Seems that way, sir."

Murdoch looked at him. "Don't tell me you're having trouble with this bit of weight? You're our Samson."

"It's not the weight, sir, it's the smell."

"Put her back then."

Crabtree started to lower the body to the ground but as he did so, Murdoch felt something in the right pocket of the woman's robe.

"Wait a minute."

He pulled out a plain envelope, unmarked and unsealed. He opened the flap and looked inside. He whistled. Stuffed in the envelope were several banknotes. Ten fifty-dollar bills, to be exact.

"That's a nice bit of dosh. Wonder where she got it?"

"From the look of her, sir, that money would have to be a lifetime's earnings."

Murdoch tucked the money into his inner pocket out of harm's way. He'd find out who had the right to it later.

"All right to put her down now, sir?"

"Fine."

"Can I open the windows?"

"Break them if you have to before we choke."

Murdoch gazed down at the corpse, to which the flies had

returned. The front placket of the nightgown was splotched with brownish stains and similar smudges were on her chin and neck. Even with all the other odours it was easy to detect the smell of beer. There was an overturned jug close beside her on the left. He picked it up and sniffed at the dregs, then he sat back on his heels and looked around. The parlour was the same size as his sitting room but contained easily twice as much furniture. The mantelpiece in front of him was black mahogany and draped with a purple satin cloth. The fender, the unwitting perpetrator of her death, was solid brass. No fire had been laid. The coating of dust was like a second skin on every surface. An oaken sideboard was against the far wall, and taking up most of the space beneath the window where Crabtree was currently breathing in fresh air was a massive roll-top desk of burled walnut. Very nobby. To the right of the door was a Turkish couch of crimson velour, partly covered with a sateen comforter. A pillow lay on the floor. He assumed this room had served as Mrs. Shaw's bedchamber. And dining room by the look of it. Dotted about the room were several used plates and dishes. One such was sitting on a nearby Morris chair and it was caked with a lemony residue that the flies were enjoying. Looked like pudding.

"Shall I send somebody for the coroner now, sir?"

"Yes, we'd better do that before she corrupts on the spot. Make sure none of those men come in until they're sworn."

The constable wrinkled his nose.

"Disgusting piece, isn't she?"

Murdoch had to agree. One can't really help loose jowls or bad teeth if she hadn't the money to fix them. Nevertheless when Crabtree had left, Murdoch made the sign of the cross over the body and said a brief prayer for the woman's immortal soul.

By two o'clock, thirteen men had been sworn for the coroner's jury and they were jammed into the tiny room. Their first job was to view the body and even with the door and windows open, the heat and smell were overpowering. Arthur Johnson was the coroner and he was showing signs of impatience. Legally the jury had to be made up of a minimum of "twelve just men and true", but as they received no remuneration most men were reluctant to serve. It meant that if they were working they would lose pay. On his first sortie into the neighbourhood Crabtree hadn't been able to find more than ten willing to be sworn. Finally he peremptorily grabbed two passersby, two brothers who happened to be walking down River Street on their way to the market. They weren't pleased but they had no choice.

"Pay attention now," said Johnson. "The sooner I get done, the sooner you can all breathe fresh air again. I'm going to point out some things to you."

The men, who had been grumbling among themselves, quieted down. Murdoch had positioned himself slightly behind the coroner's back so he could see properly. It was apparent the man next to him had recently been tucking into a meal of boiled beef and cabbage. With onions on the side. Murdoch turned around. He could see the top of Crabtree's helmet by the door. He hoped the man was all right. He still looked rather nauseous. Not that Murdoch blamed him. He, himself, was trying to breathe as shallowly as he could.

"Right now, listen carefully." The coroner bent over the corpse, pointing for emphasis as he talked. "The woman has been dead several hours. The rigidity of death which we call rigor mortis has set in completely. Notice that purple-coloured marking on her hands and feet. There, look! If you can't see move forward. You ones in front, crouch down so the others can see."

Three or four men did so.

One of the men muttered something about this being closer than he ever got to his old lady, but the responding titters were quickly squashed by Johnson's frown.

"The staining is termed lividity. It's where it should be. The blood settles in the lowest extremities and this tells us she hasn't been shifted from the position where she died. I can't turn the head, she's still too stiff. That'll start releasing fairly soon." He grinned at the men. "It's after that the fun and games begin. The skin'll turn black, maggots are everywhere, and before long not even her own child would know her."

The jurors with the more vivid imaginations shifted uneasily.

"If we roll her on her side, like so, you can see some blood on the back of her cap." He waited while they peered at the mark. "She stinks of ale. There are stains on her robe and there was a jug right next to her. I've put it on that table. There were beer dregs in it. As you can see she's lying on top of the fender. There's a tiny mark of blood there. No, it's all right, you don't have to all move. You can take my word for it. There are no obvious signs of violence on the body, the room is not disturbed. It's a disgusting mess but that's not the same thing."

Some of the men laughed, glad to relieve the tension.

"I assume therefore that the woman got herself pie-eyed, fell, and connected her head with the fender in a manner so as to crack her skull."

"Is that what killed her, sir?" asked Clarence Daly, who was one of those subpoenaed as a juror.

"That's what I'm suggesting, isn't it? Any better ideas?"

The men variously shook their heads. More than one of them had had the experience of falling down drunk.

"We'll know for sure after the post mortem examination," Johnson continued. "Now who is she? One of you must know her, surely."

"I do," said another man.

"And who are you? Speak up so the constable can write it down."

"My name's Dick Meadows. I live down the street a piece. Her name was Dolly Shaw."

"Do you know her to be a heavy drinker?" asked Johnson.

"Worse than any judge if you ask me, sir."

There was a chuckle at his little joke, but the coroner glared. "I don't want to hear any impertinence from you men. This is a serious matter."

"Sorry, sir." Meadows tugged at the brim of his hat in deference.

"Detective Murdoch here has found some money on the woman's person. Anybody know anything about that? What did she do for a living? Daly, do you know?"

"I don't think she did anything, sir," answered Daly. "Leastwise not that I saw. She has a grown daughter and she takes in washing. There are two nippers live with her but they're too young to bring in much."

An older man with a long unkempt beard spoke up. "I've lived on this street for ten years, sir. Dolly Shaw came here three years ago. There's never been a whisper that she had muck. She was always begging and borrowing from the neighbours as I heard."

There was a murmur of assent.

Johnson shrugged. "She most likely didn't want it known she had any savings. Why you people don't put money in the banks where it belongs, I'll never understand. Any questions so far?"

There weren't.

"I'll fix the inquest for Monday morning at ten o'clock. We might as well hold it at Humphrey's. That's the undertaker on Yonge Street for those of you who don't know. Just north of Wilton Street on the west side. The doctors usually like to do the post mortem examination there."

"Excuse me, sir." A broad-shouldered man with a wide, red-veined face put up his hand. "I'm on the night shift at the Dominion Brewery. I have to get my kip in or I'm a goner."

Johnson called over to Crabtree.

"Constable, how many jurors did you say we have?"

"Thirteen, sir."

"All right then, you're lucky, young fellow. Seeing as we're only required to have twelve you're excused. Everybody else, I will see you at ten o'clock. Sharp, do you hear! We'll have the doctor's report by then and anything else Detective Murdoch digs up."

The men began to shuffle out, a burst of chatter released among them. One of them accidentally trod on a plate that was on the floor. Irritably, he wiped his boot clean on the carpet. Whatever the food had been, it wasn't identifiable. Maybe mashed potatoes.

"Do you have an ambulance outside?" the coroner asked Murdoch.

"Yes, sir."

"Take the body over to Humphrey's. Let's get on promptly." He waved his hand. "This weather, the sooner we put her under the better."

Murdoch heartily agreed.

CHAPTER FOUR

THEY HAD ONLY ENOUGH MONEY FOR TWO STREETCAR tickets, so after some wrangling they agreed to ride to the house and walk back. As Annie pointed out, they would be hot and dusty and less presentable if they walked first. Privately, she hoped they might get some money out of Meredith but she didn't say that.

The streetcar let them off at the corner of Wilton and Church and they proceeded over to Jarvis, a wide, gracious street dappled with shade from the broad-leaved hawthorn trees that overhung the sides. They didn't talk to each other, and Millie dragged a pace or two behind like a sulky child. She hated being anywhere in public with her sister. Annie was wearing her best linen suit of blue-and-white check. It was sedate enough in itself but the hemline was a few inches too high and the jacket too tight. As well, the straw hat perched on her head was bedecked with dancing blue ostrich feathers and a cascade of mauve taffeta ribbons. She was carrying a red parasol.

"I do wish you wouldn't walk like that. It isn't becoming," Millie muttered at her sister's back.

It was a foolhardy thing to say because Annie stopped immediately and turned with a ferocious glare.

"Like what? How am I walking?"

Millie winced but went on. "You're swinging your parasol as if you were... well you'd think you were leading a parade."

"I'd rather walk like that than creep along like a mouse that's expecting the cat to pounce."

The contempt in Annie's tone brought tears of humiliation to Millie's eyes. But there was an awful truth in the remark and she knew it. She was wearing her good navy serge jacket and grey skirt but the clothes were out of fashion and dowdy. Her black felt hat was trimmed only with a strip of brown silk and she carried her head bent into her hollow chest.

"Why any man would want to have a bit off with you, I don't know," added Annie. At that moment, she meant what she said. Millie's unhappiness was making her look worn and frowsy.

She set off again, swinging her parasol even more jauntily. She was actually glad for the little tiff, happy to be distracted, even momentarily, from her thoughts.

However, her mind kept returning there, the way one probes

at an aching tooth. It didn't help, probably made things worse, but it was impossible to stop.

The Brogan family had not even been settled in Toronto a month when an outbreak of diphtheria snatched away both parents and two younger brothers. Annie and Millie had been taken in by a Mr. and Mrs. Reilly who were fellow emigrants. Although there were already five children in the family, the Reillys didn't hesitate. "We're poor but we'll share what we have and bring them up in the knowledge of their Faith." These proclamations were said to any who would listen and had garnered much praise and some money from the parish. In practice, it meant that the girls quickly became the household skivvies, expected to earn their keep by doing as many menial chores as Mrs. Reilly needed. Annie was seven, Millie five.

They were given a tiny room at the rear of the house which they shared with the two youngest girls. It was little more than a lean-to and in the winter it was freezing. They all suffered from colds and painful chilblains. Annie could have endured the discomfort, the hard work, but there was worse. Their room was off the kitchen where the two older boys slept. No matter how she schemed to get to bed ahead of them, one or the other, Thomas or Patrick, was usually lying in wait.

"Millie, you can go. You stink anyway. But you, pretty Miss Brogan, you we'll keep."

Annie took a deep breath, feeling the bite of her stays into her ribs.

"Annie! Annie, wait up, this is the house."

She stopped. Millie was pointing to a yellow brick house with dark green gables that sat back from the road in a well-tended garden.

"What's the matter?" she asked. "You look like a goose just walked over your grave."

"Never mind, just memories. They'll do you in every time. Let's get on with it."

Annie caught her by the arm and pushed open the gate. The wrought-iron fence was high and elegant, enclosing various tidy shrubs. All in their proper place.

Together, the two sisters went up the paved path to the front door.

"Nobby," said Annie, indicating the glass panel. It was an ornate flower design in red and green.

"Somebody's been working on this," said Annie, and she tugged at the gleaming brass bellpull with vigour.

The door opened and a young footman in grey livery stood in front of them. His polite demeanour vanished immediately.

"Millie! What are you doing here?"

"We've come to have a chat," Annie answered for her.

He stepped forward, half closing the door.

"Not here. You'll get me sacked."

"Where then?"

"Go around to the back, there by that path. I'll run and let you into the kitchen. But I can't stay more than a minute –"

"That'll probably be half a second longer than it took to put the kid in the basket."

He turned a shade of white-green.

"Oh God! No!"

"Oh God, yes."

Millie suddenly burst into tears, her nose and eyes running all at once. Annie almost felt sorry for Meredith, he was so terrified. He glanced agonizedly over his shoulder.

"I daren't talk to you anymore. Burns is a devil."

At that moment, they heard a child's voice, and a young girl about seven or eight years old appeared behind him.

"Excuse me, Meredith, we're going out."

He had to step aside and she came onto the top step.

"I beg your pardon, I didn't know we had visitors." Her manners were exquisite.

"Er, these are my, er, cousins, Miss Sarah, from the country."

"How do you do? We're going on the open-air streetcar to the lakeshore," she said, needing to tell somebody in her excitement. She turned as a woman came to the door, dressed for an outing. "Here are Meredith's cousins, Auntie. They're from the country."

The woman was of middle age, elegantly dressed, and would have been considered handsome except for her disfigurement. A wine-coloured naevus covered her right cheek, pulling up her lip so she seemed to be caught in a perpetual sneer.

At the sight of the two young women, she halted in the doorway. Her shock was palpable. Her hand flew to her face.

Meredith mistook her reaction for disapproval.

"I'm sorry, Mrs. Pedlow, they won't stay –"

She stared at him blankly. "I beg your pardon?"

Annie jumped in. "Don't worry about us, madam. We've just come for a quick visit."

The older woman suddenly pulled down her veil and started to button her gloves.

"That's quite all right, Miss, er?"

"Brogan. Annie. You might have heard of me. I'm on the stage. I sing."

Millie gave a little moan of mortification. She hadn't told John about her sister's livelihood.

Annie gestured in her direction. "This is my sister, Mildred Brogan."

"And you're related to Meredith."

"In a manner of speaking."

The footman was moving as if he had livestock in his breeches, and Millie was trying to bury herself in her handkerchief.

"May I go ahead?" Sarah called.

Both Mrs. Pedlow and Annie suddenly focused their attention on the little girl.

"Your daughter is so like you, if I may say, madam," said Annie.

"I'm told there is a likeness, but Sarah is actually my first cousin once removed. Her mother died in childbirth in England. The father had passed away earlier and as there was nobody else, my husband and I became her guardians. She is my ward."

Annie's gaze didn't waver. "How good of you to do that for an orphan."

"She has brought great joy to my life, so it has been no hardship."

Sarah hovered at the gate, afraid to go further.

"Auntie, may I go on?"

Suddenly Annie said, "Children love the theatre, don't they? I am acquainted with the manager at the opera house. Would you like me to take her down there? He would show us around."

Millie stared in horror at her sister then buried her face once more in her sodden handkerchief. Meredith gaped.

Mrs. Pedlow fidgeted with the veil on her hat. "Thank you, Miss Brogan. That is very kind." Her voice was tight. "Perhaps we could, er, talk about it first. I wonder could you call…?"

"Love to. Would tomorrow afternoon suit you?"

"Perfectly. Shall we say three o'clock?"

"Done."

Annie actually thrust out her hand as if they were two men sealing a contract. Awkwardly, Mrs. Pedlow touched the young woman's fingers. Kid glove meeting kid glove.

"Now if you will excuse me, Sarah is longing for her ride." She paused. "Meredith, please give your cousins some refreshment. It is a warm day."

"Yes, ma'am. Thank you."

Mrs. Pedlow walked away down the path, her back straight and stiff. Her silk walking suit was a lilac tint with deep flounces of airy cream lace at the throat and sleeves, the hat a huge masterpiece of lilac ribbon, flowers, and lace. The outfit would have paid the sisters' rent for several months.

"Annie, how could you be so bold?" Millie whined at her.

"Oh, Millie, shut your trap. You don't know anything. Nothing at all."

CHAPTER FIVE

SINCE THEIR NEW LODGER HAD ARRIVED, MRS. KITCHEN had set up the front parlour for meals. It meant she had to bring Arthur out into the back room but she insisted. At first, Murdoch missed the coziness of the kitchen where he'd eaten before, but he now had the chance to sit down with Mrs. Jones and her son, Alwyn, and he liked that a lot.

There was a soft tap on the door and Mrs. Kitchen came in with a tray.

"I made you a semolina pudding for your sweet."

Murdoch patted his stomach. "How am I going to compete in the games if you keep feeding me like this? I'll be having to enter the fat man's race if I carry on."

She smiled, pleased. "Nonsense. A man needs his strength." She put the tray on the sideboard. "How was the fish?"

"Delicious."

Friday was a meatless day and they'd had boiled turbot for dinner.

She placed the dish of yellow pudding in front of him and stood to watch him take his first spoonful.

"Hmm, wonderful," he said, lying blatantly.

Truth was he could have lived happily the rest of his life without ever tasting semolina again, but he wouldn't hurt her feelings by saying so.

"The boy polished his off in no time. His mother eats like a bird, though. Needs some meat on her bones."

Murdoch thought the young widow's flesh was perfect for her small stature, but again he just concentrated on getting down his sweet and made an agreeing noise.

"After you've finished, why don't you come sit out front with us. Arthur's fever has gone up so a bit of night air might do him good."

"Thank you, Mrs. K., I'd like that."

She started to gather up his dishes and said artlessly, "Would you mind to run up and ask Mrs. Jones if she'd like to join us? These days the upstairs can get to be an oven. And her working away 'til all hours. It's pleasant outside right now."

"All right."

Ever since Enid Jones had arrived, Beatrice vacillated in her opinion of the young woman. Personally, she liked her a great deal. She was sober and industrious, kept her own room spotlessly neat, took good care of her son. However, every Sunday Beatrice was forced to admit that Mrs. Jones was a Protestant. When Mrs. Kitchen set off with her rosary grasped in her hands, telling her beads on the way to St. Paul's, Mrs. Jones and her son would head in the opposite direction towards the big Baptist church on Jarvis Street. She carried a plain black Bible. On those days, Beatrice gave up the notion of matchmaking for William. During the week, however, the idea had a way of creeping back in.

Murdoch knew perfectly what his landlady was up to, but as he had the same feelings himself, voicing an objection seemed hypocritical. He pushed back his chair and wiped his moustache clean of any pudding that might be sticking there.

"I'll go this minute."

He put on his jacket, which he'd placed on the back of the chair, and blessed with Mrs. K.'s smile of approval he went in search of the widow Jones.

There were three rooms upstairs. He rented one as a bedroom and one as a small sitting room. It was a tight squeeze on his wages, but he liked having the extra space and it had helped out the Kitchens. Mrs. Jones and her son shared the front room next to him at the top of the stairs.

Her door was open to allow for a cross draft from the open window. The boy was in bed and she was sitting beside him singing softly in a lilting language Murdoch presumed was Welsh. She had lit a candle, and in the yellow light she looked softer and less worried than she did normally. Alwyn's eyes were closed. Murdoch paused at the threshold but she turned at the sound of his step. She put a finger to her lips, gave the child a gentle kiss on the forehead, and blew out the candle.

"*Nos da.*"

As she came out to the hall, she realized she'd undone the top buttons of her collar and she started to fasten them quickly.

Mrs. Jones worked at home. She had a typewriting machine and spent long hours at it, mostly copying lawyer's reports and insurance claims. When she was working, she wore round steel-rimmed glasses. They had left a red mark on the bridge of her nose, and Murdoch wanted to reach out and smooth the sore place away.

"Mrs. Kitchen has asked me to invite you down to the front porch for some cool air… it really is quite pleasant, er, have you been inside all day?"

"Mostly."

She finished fumbling with her buttons, but she'd missed one and he could glimpse the soft, pale skin of her throat.

"You'll join us then?"

"Thank you, but I really can't. I have a long report to finish by the morning."

"Half an hour won't hurt. If I may say so, you look tired."

She still hesitated, both of them standing awkwardly in the narrow, shadowy hall.

"No, truly. I must refuse."

Her voice had a musical cadence to it that he found entrancing. He lingered for a moment, hoping she would change her mind but she made a movement to go back into her room.

"Goodnight then," he said.

She gave him a shy smile. "*Nos da*. Goodnight."

Murdoch went to join the Kitchens on the front porch, taking the stairs faster than was really necessary.

Dusk was settling in rapidly and the gas streetlamps were lit, drawing dozens of moths and bugs in a dance of death around the flickering lights. Many of the street's residents were outside on their porches or steps, enjoying the summer evening. Here and there lamps glowed in the windows. Mr. Dwyer, an elderly bachelor who lived two houses up, was playing on a blow accordion and his neighbour Oakley called to him.

"Play 'Banks of Loch Lomond', will you, Tom?"

He began, slightly off-key but not so bad as to irritate any but the purists.

Next door to the Kitchens was the O'Brien family. Mr. O'Brien was a sailor and away for long periods of time, returning to spawn yet another child and off again. Mrs. O'Brien, with the eldest girl of her brood of eight, was sitting outside on her side of the common porch. Beatrice had wheeled out her husband in his wicker Bath chair, and she'd hooked up a hurricane lamp so she could see to work. She earned a bit of extra money by making things for a fancy goods store on Queen Street. Tonight she was crocheting a lace tidy.

Murdoch came out and sat down on the top step. The evening was cool, the air freshened by a breeze coming up from the lake.

"Do you mind if I have a pipe, Mrs. K.?"

She shook her head and he lit up his Powhatten and took a deep draw.

"Well then, Will, what's the other half of mankind been up to today?" asked Arthur.

Murdoch had got into the way of sharing the daily events of police life with the Kitchens, and Arthur, who was totally housebound, looked forward to these chats. It wasn't just for Arthur's sake that Murdoch discussed things, however; he'd come to rely on them himself.

He took another puff, wanting to choose his words carefully out of consideration for Mrs. Kitchen. "The big happening today was the discovery of a poor dead woman." He related briefly what had transpired at the house on River Street.

"How'd she die?" asked Beatrice.

"Fell and knocked her head most likely. It seemed as if she'd been drinking."

"We reap what we sow," said Mrs. Kitchen unsympathetically. She wasn't Temperance but she disliked excess of any kind.

"We'll know better after the post mortem examination. The inquest's on Monday."

"Did she have any family?" asked Arthur.

"A daughter. Grown woman but deaf and dumb. Might be simple as well. She ran off like a scared rabbit when we showed up."

Beatrice's fingers stopped for a moment. "I know who that is. I've seen her when I've been coming up from the market.

Has to be the same one. She's a brunette, a bit on the lanky side, middle-aged?"

"Sounds like her."

"She's not that simple. In her heart maybe but not in her head. Got the manners of a heathen but she's clever enough. She'll wrangle with the farmer's wives good as anybody. No mistaking what she means even though she don't speak." She continued with her crocheting. "Poor thing. I wonder what's to become of her." And she made the sign of the cross over her breast out of kindness.

"There are two boys living there as well," continued Murdoch. "Foster children as far as I could make out. I wanted them to go stay at the Humane Society but you'd think I was sending them to a training school for the fuss they made."

"Maybe they've already had a taste," said Arthur.

"Could be. They've grown up wild as foxes from what I can tell. Neither one can read nor write. It was the older boy who found her."

Murdoch had questioned George about the envelope in Mrs. Shaw's pocket, but he'd no explanation. According to him, they had a hard time making ends meet even though Lily worked like a donkey.

Arthur started to cough, helpless in its fierce bite. His wife and Murdoch waited until the fit subsided, pretending a calm neither one felt. Finally, Arthur lay back. He wiped away a spot of blood from his lips and dropped the piece of rag in the bucket filled with carbolic that was always beside him.

Mr. Dwyer had now moved into a slow, plaintive rendition of "Barbara Allen". Murdoch drew in more tobacco smoke and leaned back.

"Haven't heard that piece in a while. My mother used to sing it to us when I was a lad."

Sometimes, when his father was safely out of the way at sea, the four of them, his mother, sister, brother, and he, would sit around the fire mending the fishing nets. The room smelled of brine and fish and the knots were tough in the salt-stiff twine, but in those rare moments of peace he was happy. Albert played with his own piece of netting that his mother had given him, proudly mending it like the others, and his mother would teach them songs.

"My little brother always wanted a hearty sea shanty so he could shout out, 'Ho! Ho! Ho!' but me and Susanna begged for the sad ones."

He smiled at the memory.

"Mother would sing so sweetly it made us cry but we'd ask her again and again until she cried 'Mercy!' 'Barbara Allen' was one of our favourites."

Murdoch began to sing, quietly, so as not to intrude.

> *"Since my love died for me today,*
> *I'll die for him tomorrow…*
> *Her name was Barbara Allen."*

Mrs. O'Brien joined in and then Beatrice started to hum.

Up and down the street the song came floating on the air. Mr. Dwyer finished the final chorus and there was a little smattering of applause from the choristers, well pleased with themselves.

CHAPTER SIX

ANNIE WAS RELIEVED WHEN BURNS ANSWERED THE door, not Meredith. In spite of her bravado, she hadn't been looking forward to another encounter. The butler gazed down at her disdainfully.

"Mrs. Pedlow is expecting me," she said and handed him her calling card, one of the ones she had printed just the last week.

He glanced at her in surprise. "You're Miss Brogan?"

"Have been all my life unless you know something I don't."

"She is indeed expecting you."

He didn't need to finish the sentence. His expression said it all. *Why somebody like you is calling on Mrs. Pedlow, I cannot imagine.*

"Madam is in the gazebo. She asks you to join her there."

Annie was used to servants despising her and she'd long given up either fighting or placating. However, in spite of herself she still cared. She gave a haughty lift to her chin, sending the scarlet feathers bobbing.

"Where?"

Burns pointed. "Go across the grass and around by the porch. You'll see her."

Annie did as he said, irritated as her good boots sank into the soft earth. She lifted her skirt high above her ankles, aware that the butler was watching her.

The white gazebo was tucked into the far corner of the garden, and as soon as Annie rounded the porch, Maud saw her and stood up. Today she was dressed in a lilac-flowered muslin gown. The sleeves were full to the elbow, and the bodice was of white satin, embroidered with jet and green sequins. Annie would have felt honoured by such a presentation except she had the suspicion Mrs. Pedlow dressed like this on every occasion.

In spite of her fine apparel, she looked haggard, and the pallor of her skin emphasized the lividity of the birthmark.

"Please sit down, Miss Brogan," she said and ushered her into the shade of the gazebo.

Annie took one of the wicker chairs. She smiled.

"You could have knocked me over with a goose feather when you came through the door. What a surprise after all these years."

Mrs. Pedlow made no acknowledgement to this remark but said coldly, "May I offer you some refreshment? Our cook does make a very pleasant lemonade."

Annie was put out by her tone. She had been prepared to be friendly, but hurt, she became snooty.

"Pleasant lemonade would be… pleasant."

The other woman stiffened but she poured the drink. Annie accepted the glass and took her time sipping. She could feel Mrs. Pedlow's tension, sensed she was waiting for something, but Annie'd be damned if she took the lead. Let her do it. With ostentatious delicacy, she replaced the glass on the wicker tea trolley.

"I think it's going to rain, don't you? Very unpleasant, I must say."

Her hostess clasped her hands tightly in her lap and, not looking at Annie, she said, "Sarah will be back soon, so we can't waste time. We both know why you came here. Perhaps we could get straight to the point."

"And what point is that, ma'am?"

"Please, Miss Brogan, I really don't have much time."

"Pity that. I thought we could have a nice chat. About old times. However…" She began to unbutton her gloves. "Given that we're in a hurry and all that, do you mind if I ask you a quick question?"

"What is it?"

"What happened to your baby?"

George and Freddie were sitting at the kitchen table. They could have gone into the parlour but they were like songbirds who have been caged too long and don't fly to freedom even when the door is opened. Dolly never allowed them anywhere but the kitchen and their own room.

George had found a cigar butt on the street and was trying to get it to light, dropping matches recklessly on the floor.

"You're gonna get it if she sees that," said Freddie, and he gazed around uneasily as if Dolly was watching them. George punched him on the arm.

"Get it through your loaf, you nocky fool, she's not going to give it out again. Ever. She's gone to the grand silence, Fred. She's a stiff. Worm fodder."

This didn't soothe the younger boy who was biting back tears. He swung his legs against the wooden chair.

"What's going to happen to us then? And Lil? I wish she'd come back."

"Don't fret about the dummy. She'll be back, she's bunked off before."

"And us?"

"We'll be all right. Better than before, you'll see."

Freddie looked doubtful but he knew better than to argue. George puffed hard on the stinking cigar and managed to get a glow. He drew in a deep breath, coughed a bit, and sat back the way he'd seen the men do when he looked through the windows of the Yeoman Club down the road. He swung his dirty, callused feet onto the table.

Freddie waited, then he said in almost a whisper, "Do you think it was what Lil did as killed Mrs. Mother?"

"Not likely is it? You saw with your own eyes that Missus

got up. She was walking around after, wasn't she? Look!" He indicated a bruise on his forearm. "She could pinch good as ever."

"Why'd she die then?"

"She fell. She was drinking like a soldier since the afternoon. She fell down and cracked her head."

Freddie wriggled his buttocks on the chair. He always itched. The cigar had failed again and George gave up in disgust.

"Come on. We should get up the wooden hill."

The other boy shifted restlessly. "We can stay up now. Nobody'll mind. I want to wait for Lil."

"No, we've got a lot to do tomorrow."

"Like what?"

"Like we've got to see about a funeral."

"How do we do that?"

"Bloody hell, I don't know. We ask somebody." He smiled ferociously, his eyes turning. "We're family now, it's up to us. I said, come on."

Truth was that George was tired out and in need of retreating to his own lair, but had no intention of going up by himself.

He lit one of the porcelain oil lamps. Another thing they hadn't been allowed to touch.

"Here, you carry this. I'll bring the candle."

In a circle of light the boys left the kitchen, Freddie leading the way. At the foot of the stairs, he halted and shrank against George.

"What if she's going to come back?"

For answer George kicked him on the ankle. "Keep going,

you silly coon, or you'll get it from me worse than any ghost."

But it was the lights that gave him courage and the necessity of being hard in front of Freddie.

Once in their squalid bedroom, they closed the door quickly as if they could ever shut out spirits.

"Can we leave the light burning?" asked Freddie

George had every intention of so doing but he pretended to hesitate just to torment the younger boy.

"All right, you yellow belly. Anything to stop you bawling."

He turned down the wick of the oil lamp, leaving the candle stub lit. Instantly the room was filled with shadows. Both boys undressed hurriedly and jumped into bed.

"Can I sleep close, George?"

"Only if you don't fart or fidget."

"I won't, I promise."

"And if you piss in the bed, you'll get it but good."

"I won't." He pressed into George's bony back, his arms folded against his chest. They lay for a few moments then he said, "George, can I tell you something?"

"Better be good. You're spoiling my shut-eye."

"Somebody came here in the night."

"What d'you mean?"

"A woman came. I heard her. You were dead asleep but she was knocking like a thunder and woke me up."

"Probably Lily."

"She wouldn't knock on the front door."

George hesitated, not wishing to concede the point. "So what are you getting at, our Fred?"

"This woman. She and Mrs. Mother had a roaring good dustup."

"I didn't hear anything."

"The house could fall down and you wouldn't wake up," said Freddie, making a tentative joke. "They were yelling like a pair of teamsters, they were."

George shrugged. "So? Missus was always having a barney with somebody."

"What if the woman clobbered Mrs. Mother? Sent her off."

George grinned. "Good on her if she did."

"Should we tell the blues about it?"

"Tell the frogs? Have you lost a slate? It's nothing to do with us, is it? We were tucked up with Lethy, weren't we?" He thumped the other boy again. "Weren't we?"

Freddie clasped at his arm, weighing one fear against another. "There's something else."

"What? You're getting up my snout with your mithering."

"There was another person as came."

"What d'you mean?"

"I heard somebody else. A bit after."

"Must have been that same woman come back."

Freddie shook his head. "Seemed different. Mrs. Mother wasn't fumy. They went into the parlour. They was talking soft. No row, not like the first one. Mrs. Mother laughed. You know how she did."

He imitated a sort of mirthless cackle. George well knew

what he meant. Such a laugh was always followed by some punishment, swift, capricious, and severe. He remembered and unconsciously touched a deep scar on his chin where Dolly's ring had once caught him.

"George?"

"What? Spit it out for Christ's sake."

"Just after that I heard a big bump. Real loud like something fell."

"You're a dolt, my lad. We know she fell. That was the sound. Her idea pot kissing the fender." He paused. "Did you hear the cove leave?"

Freddie nodded. "A bit after I heard footsteps in the hall and the front door opened."

"How much after?"

"I don't know."

George raised his hand to slap the other boy. "Do I have to knock some sense into your thick head? How much after? An hour? Two minutes?"

"Don't hit me. I'm trying to tell you, honest I am. It was soon." He struggled to express the concept of time elapsing. "Five or ten minutes perhaps."

"Was there a carriage outside?"

"Didn't hear one."

George rolled onto his back and laced his hands behind his head.

"Did you hear Missus after that?"

"Not a peep." Freddie paused, trying to find his courage. "Do you think this cove did for her?"

"'Course not. How many times do I have to repeat it?" He punched the other boy with the knuckle of his forefinger. "She fell. The copper didn't think she'd been done in, did he? We'd be sitting in the clink answering questions, wouldn't we? Like happened to Lily."

Freddie shivered. "I think we should tell them."

"Tell them what?"

"That I heard somebody."

"No." For George, deceit was as instinctive as a blink. "It's nothing to do with us," he continued. "You was probably dreaming if truth be told. You know how you are. We won't say nothing. No need. Let the bluebottles do their own work." Suddenly, he squeezed Freddie's chin in his hand. "Cheer up, you little gawdelpus. It'll be all right. Look." He slipped his hand into a hole in his pillow and fished around. "See."

He pulled out a small bundle wrapped in newspaper. Inside were several bank notes, mostly one-dollar bills. He flapped them under the other boy's nose.

"Smell good, don't they."

"Where'd you get those?"

George explored the pillow again and removed a leather thong that had a small brass key attached to it.

"Where'd you think?"

"You pinched her money?"

"Not pinched, took back. By rights this money is ours considering all the work we've done for her. I just claimed our just wages." He fanned the bank notes. "There's almost fifty dollars. We can live like kings."

Freddie's dark eyes widened and George smiled.

"Now come on, give us a kiss and go to sleep."

Such unencumbered friendliness was so rare that Freddie wanted to cry. George turned onto his side, pulling the boy close against his back.

"George?"

"What now?"

"Say it really was some cove who did for Mrs. Mother, what if they come after us?"

"Us? Don't be so nocky. We've done nothing. Lots of coves have had quarrels with Missus, wanting the dosh they lent her. She never paid anybody back, remember? It's nothing to do with us."

"What if that cove thinks we know something?"

"But we don't, do we? We don't know anything."

He made it clear the talk was over, and Freddie didn't want to risk spoiling the momentary softness. George was probably right. Nobody had a reason to come after them. Nevertheless, he inched closer and lay with his eyes open for a long time, watching the candle flicker and finally go out.

CHAPTER SEVEN

MAUD PEDLOW WOKE WITH A START. THE FEAR THAT sleep temporarily had held at bay broke through into consciousness. She lay unmoving, watching a patch of sunlight tremble on the ceiling. Walter was snuffling beside her and she didn't want to wake him, didn't want his intrusive curiosity. He'd complained several times in the last few days that she was in a pet, liverish, moody. None of this was spoken with sympathy or an invitation to unburden herself.

Carefully she got out of the bed, soft and stale from the night. She looked down at her husband. His mouth was slightly open, his hands folded across his chest, and he hardly seemed to breathe, as if even in sleep he was wary of the world. She moved away and reached for her wrapper. The touch of the satin was a momentary comfort but she glimpsed her reflection in the standing mirror and the silver grey and lace gown seemed drab and ghost-like.

Maud had long given up regretting her marriage. She was thirty years of age when Walter proposed to her, and she was quite aware of her choices. There had been no other suitors willing to brave the bastion of her disfigurement, and her father was not wealthy enough to sweeten the lure. Walter was a widower, one year older than her own father, and she found him humourless and crotchety. However, he had social position and money, her father was ailing, and she knew that trying to live on pretensions and a tiny income with her mother was a bleak prospect. She accepted Walter's offer of marriage at once.

At the bedroom door she paused. Downstairs she could hear the household stirring as the servants began their chores for the day. The teacups clinked on the breakfast tray, the shovel clattered in the ashes of the stove. A male voice, probably Meredith's, laughed and was answered by a burst of high-pitched giggling, quickly suppressed, from the young maid, Susan.

"Do your duty," her mother whispered to her timidly the night before her wedding. "You can't afford to be haughty." That was the only instruction as to conjugal life she received, but she was grateful to Walter, she wanted to love him. She was quite prepared to be affectionate and do what married women were required to do.

On their first night together he had fallen asleep, and she assumed he was being considerate of her inexperience. The second night, he mounted her without preamble, penetrated her painfully and quickly, but complained about how difficult it was. They had attempted relations only once after that, unsuccessfully. Walter some times liked to lie beside her and take his own pleasure while looking at her naked body but even that was not often. Maud soon settled into the common rut of wives with inconsiderate husbands. She busied herself with a round of dining engagements and took undue pleasure from expensive clothes. She was always in search of new medical discoveries that could repair her face but found none.

There were no candles lit in the hall sconces, but the morning light had crept in sufficiently for her to make her way to the nursery tucked away on the third floor. Hoping the latest maid, Betsy, was not yet awake, Maud hurried up the stairs and entered Sarah's room. The child was sleeping but as Maud came over to the bed, she turned restlessly, kicking away her quilt. The room was warm and close and Maud frowned. She had asked Betsy always to keep the window open, winter or summer, but the girl said too many flies came in and at night she closed it. Maud gently pulled the quilt all the way off and placed her hand on Sarah's forehead, smoothing away the fine hair that was sticking to her cheek. She yearned to stroke the soft skin, trace the delicate arch of the dark brows, but she was afraid her touch would burn.

She had been married for nine years when she first met Henry Pedlow, Walter's nephew. He was living in Vancouver and came to Toronto en route to taking a position with a pharmaceutical firm in India. Walter was away at the time, on the circuit, but dutifully she invited Henry to stay at the house.

Before two days had elapsed she was passionately in love with him.

He was dark-haired, rather plump, with soft brown eyes that gazed on her in admiration, not seeming to notice the purple naevus, the swollen and pulled lip. He made her laugh, noticed every new gown, and seemed content to be in her company all day long. The night before he was due to depart, she had virtually asked him to be her lover. "You can stay," she had said, stumbling over her words, ashamed that she was so awkward because of course he was already staying, sleeping in the room next to hers. But he understood and had responded with warmth, kissing her deformed mouth, which no one else in her life had ever done.

When he left the following morning she remained in her room for a week, refusing food, not wanting to move from the place of memory. It was only Walter's return that made her stir. She had no wish to offer explanations for her behaviour.

They hadn't even known he was back in Toronto. There had been no telegram or letter, just a knock at the door less than a month ago. Fortunately, Walter was at his club and Sarah was doing lessons in the nursery. Maud was alone, reading in her sitting room when Burns announced him. The shock had rendered her motionless and it was only when she realized the butler was eyeing her curiously that she regained some control and was able to greet him. He too was very contained, apologizing for not giving her notice. She barely heard his excuses, as if her ears had got stopped up with cotton. He continued to prattle on about the voyage over from India, the disagreeable climate there, the savagery of the natives. Maud said almost nothing, staring at him. Initially she was unable to find the semblance of the young man he had been. He seemed wizened, too old for his years, as if his flesh were losing a battle against the dominance of the Pedlow frame. He had grown a full moustache and his hair was longer than it should have been, but neither gave the impression of vitality. It was only when she saw his slender hands that were so agonizingly familiar to her that she truly remembered, that her body remembered, and the impulse to kiss again the soft, full lips was so strong she had to stand and walk to the window.

Suddenly the door to the adjoining room opened and Betsy came in.

"Oh I beg pardon, madam, I… is there anything wrong?"

Maud stepped back and whispered angrily, "The child is too hot, give her a cool sponge-down as soon as she wakes."

The maid knew better than to protest. It was not the first time Maud had come into the nursery at the oddest hours, and Betsy was well aware she was one of a long line of servants who had proved unsuitable to take care of the little girl.

Maud hesitated, not wanting to wake Sarah at this early hour but wanting her to be up, hungry for her welcoming smile. But the maid was watching her and she left the nursery, her need squeezing at her chest.

The church bells were ringing through the city, peal after peal until only the deaf or the incorrigibly slothful could lie abed. Episcopalian were more prevalent, closely followed by the Methodist chimes and trailed by the Roman Catholic. Sinners from all denominations stirred as they were called to prayer.

William Murdoch had been up for over an hour doing his exercises. On Sundays he didn't ride, but before Mass he stripped to his singlet and drawers, pushed back the drugget on the floor of his sitting room, and did knee bends and push-ups until his muscles screamed for a respite.

Hands behind his head, he did four more squats, grunting with the effort. "Seventy-seven, seventy-eight, seventy-nine, eighty." With a gasp he collapsed on the floor. Done.

From the next room he heard Enid singing a Welsh tune that was rousing and vigorous, like a gospel hymn. He paused for a minute to listen to her but the thought of how different their beliefs actually were depressed him and he jumped up. He had ten minutes more of exercise to do before he had to wash and change into his Sunday clothes. Mrs. Jones was now singing a rather plaintive tune in English about being in the hands of Jesus. Murdoch started to run vigorously on the spot until the noise of his own breathing drowned out the song.

The leaves of the willow tree danced in the breeze, and the movement of light and shadow across her face woke Lily. She shivered. The cave where she had slept was dank, and the night had been uncomfortably cold. She didn't have enough room to stretch her legs out straight and they felt cramped and stiff. She sat up as well as she could and eased herself cautiously to the opening of her hiding place in the riverbank. She had no way of knowing if people were close by and she moved carefully until she peeked through the curtain of willow branches. The sun had disappeared behind clouds but there was enough warmth to feel good on her cold face and hands. There was nobody on the opposite bank and on this side of the river there was no path at all so she didn't fear anybody coming that way. She, herself, entered the hideaway by edging sideways close to the riverbank. She'd found the hiding place last summer when, after another beating by Dolly, she'd run off. An old willow tree had fallen into the river, and where the roots pulled out of the ground there was a hollow. The branches hid it from view and when she had crawled into the cool gloom, like a she-fox coming home, she felt safe.

She bent down and splashed water over her face and neck. Hunger had kept her awake at first, but this morning that had gone and she felt nothing except thirst. She cupped her hand and lapped the river water. For two days she had sat by the opening, crouched within the leaves, watchful. The birds were her warning, whether they suddenly took flight or continued their usual coming and going around her. Yesterday she had felt bolder and ventured out looking for wild berries. She tried not to think, but suddenly the memory would lump into her mind. Not just of the big policeman in his helmet whom she'd seen coming up the path of her mother's house but the other men in uniform from before. Their faces red and angry, shaking their fists at her when she wouldn't walk down the cold corridor to her cell. She tried frantically to make them understand, she wasn't being bad, wasn't defiant, but her sounds only seemed to anger them the more. Her mother had made it clear with gestures and a crude drawing that Lily was going to be hanged. That the gallows was in that room at the end of the corridor. But before she died, Lily would be tortured, hot pokers would be thrust in her eyes and she'd be put on a rack and stretched until all her bones were broken. Her mother had shown her a drawing in an old book. "Just like this," she thumped the page with her finger.

First women, stiff and forbidding in their dark dresses and aprons, came to take her but she fought so fiercely, they sent for the men. Two big guards roughly subdued her and dragged her into the cell. They didn't know, because she couldn't tell them, why she struggled so desperately. Finally, they tied her into a chair and put a cloth tight about her mouth to silence the screaming. After a while the matron sent for Dolly. She was shamed into soothing her daughter, and although she managed to pinch her when the matron wasn't looking, she did communicate to Lily that she wasn't going to be tortured and hanged. Yet! That if she was very, very good and did everything she was told she would be let out. And just possibly, her mother, whom she had disgraced, would take her back.

These were the memories that Lily tried to keep away. Now, her mother was dead. It was her fault and if the men came again and the judge with his white hair, she would be forced back to that place and Dolly would not save her this time. She trembled and moaned as she wiped her eyes with her wet hands.

The waiter had knocked two or three times before Henry heard him.

"Your breakfast, sir."

Henry looked at his watch, which he'd placed on the bedside table. It was almost noon. He had slept a deep, drugged sleep that left him feeling thick-tongued and sluggish. The waiter called again and he forced himself to sit up.

"Leave it outside," he shouted with a rush of anger.

He wasn't hungry, rarely was these days, just perpetually thirsty, his throat always burning. He reached over to light the lamp on the bedside table. He kept the curtains closed. He didn't want the sunlight, didn't want a reminder that life was going on outside his room, that people with futures to think of were walking on the street, talking, laughing with each other.

He got out of bed slowly and went over to the washstand. He tilted the mirror so he could get a better view, tugged off his blood-spotted nightshirt, and contemplated his naked body.

For a long time now, this had become his morning ritual. It was foolish, morbid really, because what he saw was the inexorable progress of his disease. Abruptly he dropped to his knees and clasped his hands together in prayer. He went to church on a regular basis but it was perfunctory, polite behaviour and he knew it. However, this morning he longed to reach a God who had long seemed indifferent.

"Our Father which art in Heaven, forgive me for what I have done. I am a sinner. You have punished me, Lord, and I will try to accept Your punishment as it is just. I repent. You who see into my heart, forgive me I beg, but as it be Your will and not mine. Amen."

He repeated the Lord's Prayer over and over until finally his knees ached and he was forced to get to his feet. He had achieved no peace of mind. His prayers were barren.

CHAPTER EIGHT

THE TWELVE JURORS, TOGETHER WITH FAMILY AND friends eager to witness the proceedings, were jammed into the reception room of Humphrey's. Only Tim Pritchard was impassive. He sat back, drawing on his pipe, ignoring everybody else and irritating the shirt off all of them by his air of superiority. He had served on a coroner's jury last January when a prostitute had been found strangled on the frozen lake. He considered himself an old hand at the inquest business.

Murdoch was a bit late and he slipped into the back of the room. There were no more chairs to be had, so he stood and leaned against the wall. Crabtree was serving as constable of the court, and when he entered, like schoolchildren when the teacher comes in, the spectators fell silent immediately.

The constable went over to a lectern provided for the purpose, cleared his throat, and in a booming voice, made his announcement.

"Listen here, everybody. I have a message from the coroner, Mr. Johnson. To wit." He unfolded a piece of paper and read.

> "Gentlemen, the court doth dismiss you for this time but requires you severally to appear here again Friday, on the twenty-sixth day of July instant at the seventh hour of the clock in the evening precisely, upon pain of forty dollars a man on the condition contained in your recognizance entered into."

There was a silence as the spectators tried to sort their way through the thicket of legal language.

"What's all that mean, Constable?" called out Dick Meadows.

"It means the inquest is adjourned," answered Pritchard, who was sitting in the row in front. A murmur of disappointment rippled through the crowd. "And if you don't come back you have to cough up forty bills," he added.

"Hey, sod that," said a man in front who had the muscles and language of a labourer. "I'm off on a frigging run next Friday. I don't do it, I don't get no sodding wages."

"Too bad. Then you'll have to pay the forfeit."

"Is that true, Constable?" the man asked.

"Yes, he's right," said Crabtree. "You'll have to change your shift. You've been sworn. And you there. You watch your language or you'll get a charge. There are ladies present."

The man didn't take the reprimand well. "Why's the shicey thing being postponed?"

"Because Mr. Johnson has been taken poorly, that's why. And you're in the queen's court, don't forget. I don't want to hear one more word out of your mouth. Of any kind."

"If he leaves Dolly Shaw much longer she'll be turning all of our stomachs," called out another man.

"That's no concern of yours. You're here to do your duty no matter what."

"And who'll put bread in my kid's stomach while her pa is adoing his duty? Will you?"

Crabtree bristled. "You've had your warning, Charles Piersol. One more word and you'll be held in contempt. And that surely won't feed your child."

Piersol subsided with bad grace. Crabtree picked up a second sheet of paper from the table in front of him.

"Oyez, oyez. All manner of persons who have anything more to do with this court may depart home at this time and give their attendance here again on Friday next being the twenty-sixth day of July instant at the seventh hour of the clock in the evening precisely."

The assembly began to stir, murmuring among themselves in disappointment.

"Come on then. No loitering. And don't forget, any one of

you not appearing will pay for it. Got that, Piersol?"

As they all began to disperse, Murdoch went over to Crabtree.

"What's wrong with the coroner?"

"Poor man's got the mumps. His valet came round just now. Said he looks like a chipmunk. Very painful."

"It is. I had them when I was a lad. Anyway it's just as well he postponed. I'm not getting too far with this investigation. Can't find the daughter. She's turned into a mermaid and is still swimming down to the lake. A bit more time will give me a chance to wrap this up." Murdoch regarded his constable. "You still look queasy, George. How're you feeling?"

"About the same to tell the truth, sir. Not myself at all. My belly's cramping something fierce."

"Got the trots?"

"No, sir."

"I'll ask my landlady what she recommends. She knows a lot about medicines."

The big constable did not look well. His face was yellowish and his eyes were cloudy.

"Just try to stay out of Brackenreid's way. You know how he is. He'll be having you cupped and leeched before you can blink."

Crabtree sighed. "I'm sorry this inquest was cancelled. It was giving me a chance to stay out of the station."

Murdoch laughed and clapped him on the shoulder. "Cheer up. I'll come back with something from Mrs. K. and you'll be a new man."

"I don't know about new, sir. The old one'd do for me."

Murdoch left him to gather up the papers.

"I'll see you at the station."

It was true what George said. Getting out of Inspector Brackenreid's sphere was a relief.

Murdoch was eating his lunch in the stuffy room the constables used for their meals. He spat out one of the many gristly bits from the pork pie he was munching, which tasted stale. His mug of tea was bitter, the last of the common pot, and after two sips he tipped it into the slop bucket. He felt distinctly bad-tempered. The incessant flies were maddening, his celluloid collar was chafing his neck, and he'd got some grease from the pie on his almost-new Windsor tie, blue pongee silk and a Sears catalogue special. He undid the button on his collar and loosened the tie. To hell with it. If Brackenreid came in and slapped a fine on him, he'd tell him where he could stuff it. He debated whether or not to go to the trouble of making some more tea. The water was steaming in the smoke-blackened kettle on the hob, but he'd have to get up and he didn't feel like it. He'd overdone the knee bends yesterday.

The problem was he hadn't slept well again. He'd gone to confession on Sunday, and when the priest heard about all his lustful thoughts, he'd handed out a long penance. Good thing Murdoch wasn't telling him everything.

The door opened and Constable Crabtree came in.

"There's a package for you, sir. Got the coroner's seal. Shall I put it on your desk?"

"No. Let's see. Have a seat for a minute."

"I'll stand if you don't mind, sir.

There was a curious tone to the constable's voice and Murdoch looked up at him.

"You should book off early if you have to. Get a rest."

"Yes, sir."

As nobody got paid for time off, most of the men struggled into work no matter what their ailments. However, they both knew Crabtree would be excused with pay if it meant he remained fit for the tournament.

Murdoch opened the envelope. There was a note from Johnson.

Murdoch. I've come down with the mumps, which means I have to postpone the inquest. Given what Dr. Ogden has to say, it's probably just as well. You've got some work to do. I've reset the inquest for this coming Friday. Should be right as rain by then. Damned painful.

Your servant, Arthur Johnson.

Curious, Murdoch turned to the handwritten sheet which was enclosed.

This is to certify that I, Julia Ogden, a legally qualified physician in the city of Toronto, did this day make a post mortem examination upon the body of a woman identified as Dolly Shaw with the following result.

The body is that of a well-nourished woman about fifty or sixty years of age. Rigor mortis and staining well marked.

General condition. Adiposity well developed.

Heart in good condition.

Liver, soft and pale, markedly fatty.

Abdominal organs, kidneys normal in size and odour.

The woman showed signs of having borne a child.

There is a one-inch contusion on the occiput but it is relatively small, the dura mater beneath is not depressed or the brain ruptured. It is highly unlikely this would have been the cause of death. There was recent bruising on the shin bone of the left leg three inches below the patella. There was also a large bruise on the right forearm, five and one half inches from the wrist. This contusion had an odd criss-cross pattern, which having examined the dead woman's outer garment, to wit a flannel robe, I decided this bruise had been incurred by pressure on the arm. Considering the discovery I made on further examination, I would now posit that this bruise was the result of some person pinning down the dead woman, probably by kneeling on her arm.

Murdoch read that bit again. The doctor was sounding unnecessarily dramatic to him. However, the next sentence said otherwise.

I discovered traces of foreign material lodged in the nasal passages, although some had been ingested deep into the

90

lungs. These traces were green in colour and under the glass seemed in my opinion consistent with a material such as cotton or wool. Perhaps more likely wool. Given the position of the body, the woman could not have smothered by accident. I have to conclude therefore that she died from forceful suffocation, likely from a person holding a cloth or pillow over her face. I am yours truly,

An illegible signature followed.

"Damnation! I missed it, Crabtree."

"Sir?"

"I was only too ready to assume she was some old sot who'd conked her head."

He told him what the doctor had written and Crabtree shrugged sympathetically.

"Don't blame yourself too much, Mr. Murdoch. That's what we all thought. Including the coroner."

"I should have been more thorough."

"Don't know what you would have found. You couldn't look in her throat," said Crabtree reasonably.

"Johnson wants a report by Friday. Let's hope those two boys haven't turned the place upside down and there's still something to investigate."

"Do you think somebody knew about her money and was intending to rob her? They might have got panicky when they realized she was done for and scarpered off?"

"Pretty thick-headed robber if that's the case, but it's not out of the question."

He stuffed his remaining piece of pie into a tin kept for the purpose so it would be safe from the mice. He was angry with himself. Brackenreid would love the opportunity to find fault, he always did. He'd never been happy with having Murdoch foisted on him. One of Stark's new men and a Papist to boot. More than that, however, Murdoch was dismayed at his own complacency.

"Let me talk to this doctor, then we'll go over there."

The constable shifted his feet and winced.

"You all right?" Murdoch asked him. For answer Crabtree's eyes rolled back in his head and with one smooth, unbroken motion he fell backwards. Murdoch was irrepressibly reminded of a Douglas fir crashing to the ground in the forest.

The constable had come around quickly, refused to go home, but agreed to stay in the off-duty room for a little while longer. Fortunately, Brackenreid was out at a fire-hall inspection and couldn't make a fuss. Murdoch left Crabtree perched on a chair sipping fresh tea and went into the outer office. A young constable, second class, was manning the telephone and telegraph.

"Call up one-three-seven-eight for me, will you, Phillips."

The constable plugged in his wire and dialled the number. The call was obviously answered immediately.

"Just a minute please, a caller for you from number-four station." He indicated the telephone to Murdoch, who put the receiver to his ear and bent down to speak.

"Hello?"

"Yes," said a female voice. "What can I do for you?"

"I'd like to speak to Dr. Ogden."

"This is she."

Murdoch felt a flash of impatience.

"Nurse, please put me through to the doctor. I'm in a hurry."

"And so am I, sir. Will you state your business? This *is* Dr. Ogden to whom you are speaking."

Murdoch shot a quick glance at the sheet of paper in his hand. He'd not paid attention to the preamble. The physician's name was Julia.

"I, er, beg your pardon, madam, er, doctor –"

She cut him short but there was amusement in her voice. "That's quite all right. I'm used to it. Dr. Stowe and I are a minority of two in this city. We are constantly being mistaken for our nurses. However, I assume you have not called to discuss the challenges I face being a lady doctor."

"Not today, ma'am, although I'm sure it is a fascinating tale. My name is Murdoch, William Murdoch, and I'm acting detective at number-four station. I just received your report on the post mortem examination of Dolly Shaw."

"Yes?" The doctor's voice was wary, expecting criticism.

"You mention a small contusion at the back of the head. Do you think it happened before or after she was smothered?"

There was a pause at the other end of the line, then she said, "What is your point, Mr. Murdoch?"

"If Mrs. Shaw fell, hit her head on the fender, and then was suffocated, it wouldn't be that hard to do. But she was a heavy woman. If she was overpowered, suffocated, then dragged to the fender in an attempt to disguise the murder, her assailant would have to be strong."

"A man, then."

"Possibly, although some women are equal in strength to men."

She laughed. "A hit, sir, a palpable hit. Frankly, it is impossible to determine whether the injury occurred very shortly after death or very shortly before. There is little bleeding."

"Could the blow have rendered her unconscious?"

She sighed. "I wish I could be more definite but I'm afraid I cannot say. She had so much liquor in her stomach, I would think she was staggering drunk. An easy pushover – literally. She may have fallen and banged her head on the fender, been dazed, and… well, I suppose her assailant could have taken advantage of that. Her gown, by the way, was splattered with beer, but from the pattern, I'd say the liquor was thrown down on her rather than she herself spilling it. Perhaps to reinforce the notion of her inebriety."

"Dr. Ogden, if you get tired of medicine you could be a consultant for the police force."

"Not very likely, Mr. Murdoch. I've met Colonel Grasett. I don't think he would believe a word I said."

Privately Murdoch thought the police chief had difficulty accepting anything anybody said, other than himself, but he didn't say so. He didn't want to overstep the mark and get too comradely with the lady. He was enjoying the conversation so far.

"Mr. Murdoch? I'm sorry I've not been of much help."

"You have, ma'am. Whatever the sequence, this was deliberate murder."

"That I concur with."

She said her goodbye and hung up. Murdoch replaced the receiver on the stand. She must be quite young because it was only recently that lady doctors could be licensed. He wondered what she looked like.

CHAPTER NINE

CONSTABLE ROBERT WIGGIN WAS THE ONLY OFFICER available to assist, and Murdoch wasn't happy about it. He didn't like or respect the man. Wiggin was sallow-faced and lanky, with a caved-in chest that no amount of reprimand from Seymour the duty sergeant could straighten. He bullied the unfortunates who ended up in the jail, but was smooth as butter around his superiors. If the inspector were to ask for an arse wipe, the constable would have done it.

Murdoch set a brisk pace over to River Street, and he took a rather mean pleasure in the fact that the constable was quite winded when they reached the corner.

The house looked abandoned, all the curtains drawn, the

black ribbon on the door drooped.

"Stand back a bit, will you, Wiggin, don't want to scare them into next year."

Murdoch thumped hard with the knocker and after a few minutes the door was opened a crack. A pair of frightened eyes peeked out at him.

"Hello, Freddie, isn't it? Can I come in?"

The boy nodded and stepped back. George appeared behind him. He too looked afraid, although he had more air of bravado than the younger lad. Murdoch entered the hall, which reeked of cigars.

"We've got to have a talk, my bravos. Kitchen?"

Freddie glanced quickly at George, who nodded. Both boys were even more unkempt than before. Murdoch followed them into the kitchen, which was lit by a single candle on the pine table. The stub end of a cigar sat in a used plate. He wondered how they had been taking care of themselves and he felt guilty that he hadn't given them more thought.

"Has Miss Lily come back yet?"

George answered. "No, we haven't seen hide nor hair of her, have we, Freddie?"

The boy shook his head.

Murdoch paused. He didn't know how to proceed. He didn't want to shock them unnecessarily.

"Boys, I want you to tell me the truth. No con, do you hear? On your honour, so help you God."

They stared at him.

"The night your foster mother died, was there any kind of barney? Did she and Lily have a set-to, for instance?"

They both tensed but George said, "They was always having rows. Never stopped, did it, Freddie? She went at Lily terrible."

"Did Lily fight back?"

"Sometimes."

"Did they go at it Thursday?"

"Don't remember."

"Freddie, what about you?"

"Don't remember," he whispered.

"Did anybody else come in to visit? A neighbour for instance? Late I mean."

"We was in bed, sir. Fast asleep."

"So your answer is no or don't know?"

"Don't know, sir."

Murdoch pushed aside the plate with the cigar. "I'm asking because we've got new information about the way Mrs. Shaw died."

"She fell didn't she, sir? And topped her noggin."

"That's what we thought, George, but it's not true. I'm afraid somebody killed her."

"Done in?" George gasped.

"Yes, done in."

"How?"

"She was suffocated."

"On purpose?" Still uncomprehending. Or pretending to be.

"Yes, on purpose. Probably with some kind of pillow. That's

why I'm asking you if anybody had a barney with her. If you heard anything."

He gave them a chance to answer but they both stared at him, looking frightened, especially Freddie.

"I'm going to have a look in the parlour in a minute. See what I can find. Have you been in there?"

Again the vigorous shaking of heads. Believable this time. Murdoch stood up. "If you do remember anything, I want you to come straight down to the station and tell me. And when Lily comes back you've got to make her understand that we need to talk to her. Can you do that?"

"Yes, sir. We will, won't we, Freddie?"

At the door Murdoch hesitated. "How are you boys managing? Have you got work yet, George?"

"No, sir. I'm going out tomorrow to look. They always needs bun boys down at the stables. I'll try there."

Again Murdoch wished he had taken more care. Freddie was a child and George not much more.

"Come and see me next week if you haven't got anything."

He went back to the front door. The constable had positioned himself at the bottom of the steps, in guard position.

"Start having a look around the front and back of the house, will you, Wiggin."

"Yes, sir." He hesitated. "What exactly am I looking for, sir? I haven't been on this sort of investigation before."

Murdoch waved him off. "Use your brain, Wiggin. Wake it up. Collect anything you think might have relevance."

He went back into the dark hall and over to the parlour. A waft of rotten air hit him as he entered the room. Most of the odour came from the dishes that were still sitting where Dolly had left them, with leftover food on them. The boys were certainly telling the truth about not coming in here. It was untouched since he'd last been.

Given what he now knew, the Turkish couch took on a new and sinister aspect. There were two pillows, one brown, one emerald green. He picked up the green one, which was on the floor. The cover was knitted and the words *Love Conquers All* were oversewn in red. He replaced it gingerly. He'd take it in to Dr. Ogden to examine. The grimy sheet on the couch was rumpled and the sateen comforter was half off, dragging on the floor. He couldn't tell if that was an indication of a struggle, however, or just of an untidy housekeeper. He began to inch slowly around the room, studying everything with new eyes.

The second Morris chair by the hearth had served as Dolly's wardrobe. Her skirt, a black cotton lined with canvas, and her grey silk waist, very stained, were draped across the back of the chair. He moved them aside. Underneath were her undergarments. Somewhat squeamishly, he gave them a cursory examination. There was a pair of stays, most of the laces broken and knotted, a white underskirt, and a pair of dirty drawers. No stockings.

He tried the desk but it was locked and he left it for the moment. Next to it in the corner was a triangular glass-fronted hutch, and he opened it up. The shelves inside were bare, no display of fine china dishes or glassware here. The dust was thick enough to write a letter in, but nobody had been that helpful. He moved on. The window that faced River Street intervened. The flowered velvet curtain was closed and he lifted the corner to peek outside. The street was deserted, but he fancied that at the same time he had lifted his curtain a neighbour across the road had dropped hers. He returned to his task.

The top of the sideboard was covered with figurines of various sizes, all nestling in dust balls. At one end was a gilt birdcage, empty, at the other a pitcher and bowl. The pitcher was half filled with water and inevitably was now the swimming hole for several flies, some still struggling. Next to it was a dish crusted with the remnants of what was once some kind of stew, and beside that two empty glasses. He opened the right-hand drawer of the sideboard. It was empty. So was the left drawer and the lower cupboards. Mrs. Shaw seemed to have preferred to have furniture for show rather than function. Given the poverty of the house itself, these pieces were quite swell.

The japanned side table by the couch told him nothing except that Dolly did not have a green thumb. The fern in its brass pot was wilting badly. He reached for the pitcher and watered the poor plant, flies and all. That left the desk. He went out to the hall.

"George!"

As fast as a jack-in-the-box, the boy's head popped through the kitchen door.

"Yes, sir?"

"I want to have a look in the desk here but it's locked. Any notion where the key is?"

George shook his head. "No, sir. We never went in Missus's room. Weren't allowed."

Murdoch returned to the parlour, almost ready to retch at the foul air. He took out a clasp knife from his pocket, opened the blade, and pried open the lock. It yielded easily. He rolled back the curtain top. The inside was nearly bare: a blotting pad, well used, an inkwell with the top off, and a steel pen. Sitting on top of the blotter was an empty tin that had once held Frey's Homeopathic Cocoa. There was no lid. At the rear of the desk was a large jar, containing what looked like herbs. There was a label, torn and faded, the writing almost illegible. He could just make out the word *Comfrey*. The cubbyholes were all empty, and all that was in the two drawers was a bag of boiled fruit candies that had melted together. He lifted the blotter and underneath was tucked a piece of notepaper. It was good quality, thick and creamy, but the edge was ragged, as if it had been torn from a book.

There was no salutation, but in large letters was written,

I'm sure you remember the occasion of our first meeting. I have had some family troubles which has forced me into changing my name for reasons of privacy as I am sure you of all people can understand. I did as good by you as I could. Times are hard, my business has fallen off. A small gratuity would be kindly received. Or else

The letter stopped there. Murdoch read it through again. The threat of the last two words was intriguing. Had it been written recently or was it of the same vintage as the candies? He couldn't tell. What was her business? The neighbour said she didn't do anything and that her daughter supported them. What were her family troubles and did any of this have to do with her murder? The letter cast a different light on the money he'd found in Dolly's pocket. Was she into blackmail? Maybe the five-hundred dollars was pay-off money? People with something to hide can get desperate if threatened with discovery.

There were two banks of drawers on each side of the desk and he pulled them open. Dolly had used this piece of furniture as her pantry. In every drawer was some food: stale bread, mouldy cake, a piece of black meat crawling with maggots.

He was just about to close up the bottom one when he glimpsed the end of a calling card sticking out from beneath a saucer that had found its way into the drawer. He plucked it out. In plain black lettering was the name *Mrs. Walter Pedlow*. The cardboard was bent and dirty but of good quality stock. He frowned. The name had unpleasant associations for him. Walter Pedlow was a judge, and Murdoch had been a witness in his court a few years ago. Pedlow had seemed harsh, erratic, and of great personal vanity, an unfortunate combination of qualities in a judge. What was Dolly Shaw doing with the calling card of his honour's wife? He put both the letter and card in one of the envelopes he'd brought with him and stowed it in his pocket. On an impulse, he shook out some of the herbal mixture that was in the jar and also put that in an envelope. Finally, he pulled out some of the threads from the emerald pillow and saved them.

For the next several moments, he stood looking around the room, trying to read the story of what had happened. But there were still too many variables and he felt frustrated with them.

He went back to the kitchen.

George and Freddie were at the table, not doing anything that he could see, except waiting.

"Come on, boys. I have to look upstairs and you might as well come with me."

Mutely, they followed him up the stairs to the landing. There were two doors, both closed.

"Whose is whose?"

"That's ours," said George, pointing to the one on the left.

"Come on then, open up."

George opened the door and Murdoch stepped into the small bare room. There was a narrow bed against the wall, a washstand, and a chair. Nothing else.

"Excuse me, sir," Freddie said timidly. "But could I ask you what you're looking for?"

Murdoch grinned and ruffled the boy's hair.

"Anything that don't belong."

Freddie looked puzzled. "Nothing belongs really, sir. Was all Mrs. Mother's."

George didn't say anything. His turned-in eyes made it difficult to read his thoughts.

"All right, next room. Is that one Miss Shaw's?"

"Do you mean Lily?" asked Freddie.

George thumped him hard on the arm. "Don't be so nocky. 'Course that's who he means."

The boys behind him like an entourage, Murdoch went across the landing and opened the door to the other room. In the bright morning light the little chamber seemed almost cheery. The quilt on the bed was colourful, the edge of the huckaback towel on the washstand was crocheted in white, and another doily covered the top of the small dresser.

"Wait here, boys."

He closed them out. It seemed more respectful to give the absent woman the dignity of a private search. He started with the dresser which, like the furniture downstairs, was good oak. The mirror was missing but otherwise it was in excellent condition. He was curious about the objects that were placed on it. In the centre was a black marble clock. Once probably beautiful, it no longer had hands and only two bits of the coloured inlay were left on the facing. Beside it was a china dog, about six inches high. The eyes were blank and most of the nose was gone as if in some fierce fight. It sat lopsidedly because it had no rear leg but there was a clean, red ribbon around its neck. He replaced it carefully. On the left side of the overbearing clock was a posy of field daisies in a cracked crystal vase. Lily had obviously collected discarded treasures, attempting to make beauty bloom in the barren desert of her life.

He pulled open the top drawer of the dresser. It contained

a plain flannel nightgown, a woollen undervest, and two pairs of black knitted stockings, neatly rolled up. He felt around the edges of the drawer. There was something underneath the clothes. He lifted out the nightgown, and lying underneath it was a black leather-covered book. The pages were edged in gilt and the lettering was red and gold. *The Royal Path of Life*, illustrated by the Reverend Potts. A serious and portentous tome, "Designed to elevate the tone, purify the heart, and strengthen the character of all who accept its teachings." The book was pristine, but he didn't know if it was buried beneath Lily's nightgown because she considered it precious or useless. He turned to the frontispiece, which was protected by tissue paper. There was a stamp below the title: "Awarded to Lily Merishaw for perfect attendance at Markham Village Sunday School, December 1864." That was thirty-one years ago. He could hear the two boys whispering together outside. He opened the door. They were sitting on the floor.

"Did your foster mother ever use another name that you know of?"

"Like what, sir? What sort of name?"

"Merishaw. Did she ever call herself Dolly Merishaw?"

George shook his head. "Don't remember that, sir."

"Freddie? Do you?"

"No, sir."

"What about Lily? Did she ever refer to herself as Lily Merishaw?"

George grinned. "She don't talk, sir. Only grunt like the pigs.

She don't read nor write neither."

"All right. You two can go back downstairs. I'm almost done here."

Murdoch returned to the dresser and replaced the book where he'd found it. The second drawer held only a clean pair of undergarments and a cotton corset cover. What other clothes Lily had, she must have been wearing. The pitcher on the washstand was filled, the chamber underneath the bed was empty. It was highly likely that the woman was the perpetrator of a violent crime against her own mother, but standing here in this neat room Murdoch felt more compassion than disgust. He had the sense of a person striving for some betterment. The contrast with the refuse pile that her mother had lived in was striking.

As he went downstairs to join George and Freddie, Constable Wiggin entered.

"I've searched the yards, sir. Can't say I found anything special except this cigar snip."

He handed his prize to Murdoch.

"Where was it?"

"Near the gate. Seems quite fresh."

Murdoch placed it in his remaining envelope. Given the crowd of onlookers who'd been hanging around the house, the snip probably came from one of them, but he wanted to be thorough.

"I'm almost done here. Just got to have a look around the kitchen. Why don't you start talking to the neighbours. Go down River Street. I'll go across the road."

"Yes, sir. Anything in particular I should ask them?"

"Nothing in particular. Just if they are the one who smothered Dolly."

"Yes, sir."

"Wiggin, wait. That was a joke. An attempt at humour."

"Oh, I see."

"Ask them if they heard anything on Thursday night. Find out what they were doing, what they felt about the dead woman. That sort of thing."

The constable left and Murdoch wondered again why the man had chosen a career in the police force. His kind gave everybody a bad name.

CHAPTER TEN

NEITHER THE KITCHEN NOR THE CELLAR HAD GIVEN OUT any new information, and Murdoch walked across the road to start his questioning with the neighbours directly opposite. The ones who had shown interest in what he was doing earlier.

The trim on the house opposite was freshly painted in a popular dark green, and there were lace curtains at the windows. Both the brass door knocker and boot scraper showed evidence of diligent polishing. A house-proud woman lived here. It was she who opened the door, a plump, short woman, plain and neat in brown taffeta. He explained who he was and with a flurry of excitement, she showed him into the front parlour and went to fetch her husband. He was John Golding and she was his wife, Mary, she said breathlessly.

Mr. Golding was stocky, of middle age, and like his wife neatly and soberly dressed. The startling thing about him, however, was that his face and neck were covered with white, fungus-like tubercles. Murdoch couldn't help his own reflexive reaction to look away.

"I was just about to make a pot of tea, Mr. Murdoch. Can I bring you one? Or would you prefer coffee?" said Mrs. Golding, providing a distraction while her husband seated himself.

"Tea would be splendid," replied Murdoch, also welcoming the diversion.

Mary Golding had shown him into their parlour, as neat and sober as the couple themselves. Murdoch had the impression of brown everywhere. The lace curtains cut down on the light, and given Mr. Golding's appearance, he wondered how much that was deliberate. Golding spoke first. His voice was hearty and resonant.

"No need to be embarrassed, Detective Murdoch. I'm used to people shying away. I've had these growths for going on five years. God in His wisdom has seen fit to try me."

"Is there anything can be done?"

"I stopped going to doctors years ago. They all wanted to have sketches made of me for one of their textbooks. That or get me to come down to the medical school as an exhibit for the young men. No thank you. This affliction came and it'll go when God wants it to."

Murdoch's gaze was steadier now, and he could see weariness and pain in Golding's eyes in spite of his pious words. He wondered how his wife tolerated God's affliction. At that point, she came back into the room. If the dreadful growths bothered her she gave no sign.

"Here you are, Mr. Murdoch."

She must have quickly taken out the best china because his cup and saucer were of a fine pattern and light as an eggshell. The tea was strong and rich, much more palatable than the brew at the station. He took some sips and waited to allow Mrs. Golding to settle like a timid bird back into her nest.

"The reason I'm here is to ask you both a few questions about Mrs. Shaw, your neighbour. As I'm sure you know, she was found dead on Thursday last."

They nodded. Mr. Golding's tuberous growths actually swayed. Murdoch was reminded of sea anemones.

"I regret to say that according to the doctor who conducted the post mortem examination, Mrs. Shaw didn't die from natural causes. She met with foul play."

Golding clicked his tongue. "Doesn't surprise me."

"Why is that?"

He leaned forward and Murdoch tried not to flinch. "Me and Mrs. Golding here are strong churchgoers, Baptist. Dolly Shaw never set foot in any church that I know of." He paused and glanced over to his wife. "Mary, perhaps you could warm up the pot for us."

"But John –"

"Mary, if you please," he said, and with a little sigh of resignation she left the room.

When the door had closed behind her, Golding continued with lowered voice.

"Lots of times my whole body aches something fierce and it keeps me awake. Many a night I've just sat in Mary's rocker there and watched the sun come up." Another pause. Murdoch noticed that Golding's hands were afflicted with the growths as well.

"I've seen people coming and going over at Dolly Shaw's house when all law-abiding Christians should be home in their beds. And I tell you, Officer Murdoch, those people are all of the female kind. All women and none of them Christian, believe me."

Murdoch wasn't completely sure what he was getting at. Golding saw his frown.

"To put a blunt tongue on it, Mr. Murdoch, that woman used to be a midwife, and she no doubt knows all sorts of ways to help those godforsaken women out of their trouble. That's what they go to her for, you mark my words. And if there's one kind of murder going on, you're paving the way for another. That's why I said I wasn't surprised."

He tapped the side of his nose with his forefinger. "The woman also drank like a guardsman. Every day, the daughter, poor woman, or one of those benighted boys would bring her jugs of beer. They'd get it cheap from the Dominion Brewery on Queen Street there. Must have been stale as a beggar's crust."

He eyed Murdoch speculatively. "Mrs. Golding and me are

Temperance." For a minute Murdoch thought he was going to demand to know if he'd taken the pledge, but he forestalled the question with one of his own.

"Did you happen to see anybody coming or going last Thursday night?"

"Certainly did. That night was a bad one. I was burning like I'd been dipped in acid. I was seated right here in the rocker, trying to get some peace, when I seen a young woman come. About midnight, I'd say. Maybe just after. She started pounding on the door over there without any care that law-abiding folks was in their beds."

Quickly Murdoch took out his notebook and pencil.

"What did this woman look like?"

"She was wearing one of those waterproof cloaks, although there was not the smidge sign of rain. Trying to disguise herself she was. Didn't fool me. I saw her face when she passed under the light. I recognized her at once. She's a singer down at the Derby on Queen Street."

"How'd you know?"

"Tuesday last I was at that tavern." He smiled. "Don't misunderstand me, Mr. Murdoch, I was doing a bit of preaching. Outside. They won't let us in, of course. Me and a couple of fellows and ladies from the league go out regularly to the taverns."

"Have any luck?" Murdoch couldn't help interjecting.

"Oh, yes. Why just two weeks ago I had this young fellow on his knees praying with me. He signed the pledge there and then. Said he was a married man and a father and the demon drink was destroying him. As it does, officer, as it does."

He looked as if he was about to launch into a speech.

"Could you continue with what you were saying about the woman?"

"Yes, well, me and Miss Yielding were working that night. She's a mighty fine speaker when she gets going, can reel 'em in like sprats on spawning day. Turned out the young woman in question was performing at the Derby." He snorted. "I dignify it by saying performing. All she does is wear skimpy clothes and sing suggestive songs. Don't take much talent to do that, does it?"

"I suppose not."

"Anyways, just as we got there and was handing out our leaflets at the door this one waltzes by. Big hat with red feathers and a red striped dress revealing as much as Mother Nature ever gave her if you ask me. Miss Yielding stepped forward to give her a leaflet. She took it, glanced at it, then laughed out loud and tossed it to the ground. Rude as you like. Well, my companion was a bit affronted by this, and so she should have been. She came at that daughter of Eve again but she shoved her aside. I mean shoved, like she was some kind of ruffian. Poor Miss Yielding fell down. Wet it was that night, and she fair ruined her skirt."

"You're sure it was the same woman who came to see Dolly?"

"Sure as a judge. I told you, I saw her clearly when she passed under the streetlamp."

"Did she go in the house?"

"She did. I watched. I must confess to being a bit curious as our paths had already crossed as it were."

"Did you see her leave?"

Golding paused. "To be God honest, I did not actually see her. I had taken a sleeping draught, and wouldn't you know, it sent me off soon after that Jezebel arrived. But I did wake up about two by the clock there. I heard footsteps skittering down the street as if the Devil himself was snapping at her heels. Which he probably was, given what she'd done."

"We don't know that for certain, Mr. Golding," protested Murdoch. "What direction did the steps go in?"

"She headed off westerly along Wilton."

"Same way as she came?"

Golding hesitated. "Couldn't swear on the Holy Book about that. She might have, might not. But it isn't important, surely? If she came one route and went back another, she's still one of the damned."

"Do you know her name?"

"I do indeed. After she had treated Miss Yielding so badly we asked one of the customers going into the Derby. Annie Brogan is who she is."

There was a tap on the door and his wife poked her head in.

"Can I come in now?"

"Yes, we're all done, my dear."

Murdoch wasn't quite sure why Mrs. Golding had been banished, whether it was from delicacy given what her husband had told him or whether Golding was the kind of man who didn't believe in the woman participating in manly talk.

He stood up. "Thank you for the tea, Mrs. Golding. It hit the spot."

"Are you off to speak to that young woman?"

"I am."

He gathered freshening up the teapot wasn't all she'd been doing.

"Mr. Murdoch, is there anything I can do for those two boys?"

"The house is in sore need of a clean-up, but we're sort of stymied until Mrs. Shaw's daughter returns. There can be a funeral as soon as she claims the body. In the meantime..." He shrugged.

"I'll just keep an eye on them for now. I believe Lily has vanished like this before. She just seems to wander back eventually."

Golding shook his head. "What's the world coming to? By the way, Mr. Murdoch, I assume you yourself have taken the pledge."

"Won't touch a drop when I'm on duty," replied Murdoch ambiguously, and he picked up his hat and left quickly.

CHAPTER ELEVEN

JUST DOWN FROM THE STATION, ON PARLIAMENT STREET, there was a pharmacy and Murdoch headed there first. The bell tinkled as he opened the door and stepped into the dark interior. The shop smelled of camphor. The druggist was standing behind the counter, which was laden with bottles filled with variously coloured liquids. He had large, prominent ears, twinkling eyes, and looked rather like an elf among woodland flowers. He smiled the happy welcome of somebody who hasn't seen many customers this morning. The nameplate on top of the counter said *Mr. Bright*.

"What can I do for you, sir?"

"I'm William Murdoch, acting detective at number-four

station. Wonder if I could ask you a couple of questions?"

Mr. Bright's smile dimmed slightly. Not a paying customer then. However, curiosity made him cheer up.

"Ask away. Only too glad to be of service."

Murdoch took out the envelope from his pocket and gave it to the druggist.

"I wonder if you can tell me what this is?"

Mr. Bright shook out some of the mixture into his hand. He sniffed carefully, turned his head away to breathe, then smelled the substance again. Delicately, he took a pinch, rubbed it between his fingers, and tasted it. Repeated that. Finally he took a magnifying glass out of the drawer and examined the herbs. He frowned.

"Am I allowed to ask why you want to know?"

"I'm investigating a serious criminal case."

Bright nodded solemnly. "I can imagine what." He dusted off his palm. "There's a hint of liquorice smell, which means the herb pennyroyal. The woody bits are cottonwood bark by the look of it, and the green slivers are tansy. I'd have to do some proper tests if you want me to swear on oath, but I'd say that's what we've got."

Murdoch had suspected as much. They were abortifacients.

"Would these herbs be easy to come by?"

"Easy as roses. You can order a mixture like this from the Sears catalogue or you can grow them yourself. You have to know the right proportions, mind you, but there's lots who'll tell you for a bit of Judas money."

Murdoch wondered if the herbs were the reason for Dolly's late-night visitor. And if they had anything to do with the money on her person or her death.

"Thank you, Mr. Bright. You've been a great help."

For a moment, the druggist looked sorrowful.

"It's a tragic thing that young women are driven to such measures."

"Indeed."

He left the man to his ruminations and set off for the Derby.

The tavern was a narrow three-storey building sitting at the corner of King Street and Parliament, just far enough away from the grand shops not to contaminate them. There was a foundry to the left on King Street whose tall chimneys were puffing out dark, acrid columns of smoke, like a warning of hellfire. The imbibers in the tavern seemed oblivious to any such message, and as Murdoch approached he could hear the noise of raucous singing.

> *"Daisy, Daisy, give me your answer do.*
> *I'm half crazy all for the love of you..."*

All of the tavern windows were up and smudges of tobacco smoke drifted out towards the street. He propped his wheel against the curb, watched idly by a small knot of men who had spilled outside and were clustered around the doorway. They yielded reluctantly as he pushed his way through and went into the tavern. The thick fug that assailed him made his eyes sting and he coughed. The room was jammed, mostly with working men. A line of choristers was standing on the benches, arms linked, pints in one hand, pipes in the other. They were swaying back and forth and singing their lungs raw.

> *"It won't be a stylish marriage.*
> *I can't afford a carriage…"*

The mob was so dense he couldn't get any further into the room, but he could see a stage at the far end with two limelights illuminating a young woman perched atop a stepladder. A board to the right of the stage announced that she was *Miss Annie Brogan: Internationally Acclaimed Chanteuse*. If she was a good singer Murdoch couldn't tell at this point because her voice was totally drowned out by her audience.

> *"I can't afford a carriage…"*

Miss Brogan descended step by step from her ladder, her skirt hitched sufficiently to show off a dainty white boot and the edge of lace drawers. She came to the front of the stage and leaned forward, revealing a generous amount of naked, rounded flesh flowing over the top of her well-cinched bodice. Her bare arms gleamed in the white light.

"Keep going," she called out.

> *"You'll look sweet upon the seat of a*
> *bicycle made for two."*

Murdoch began to shoulder his way through the crowd so he could get closer.

"Hey you, where's your ticket?"

A burly man in shirtsleeves who was stationed near the door grabbed him by the arm.

"I don't have one," said Murdoch.

"Thirty-five cents."

He could have fished out his identification card but he decided not to. He would rather get the lay of the land first. Knowing he was a detective had a way of changing people's normal behaviour.

He managed to get some money out of his pocket and handed it to the doorkeeper. They were standing so close their noses were only a few inches apart.

"Here. Hold on to it. No spitting and no climbing on the stage unless you're asked."

Nobody else seemed to have paid attention to either rule. The straw-strewn floor was sticky with spilled beer and expectorations of tobacco juice, and Murdoch noticed two young mashers in striped blazers were trying to get on the stage. The doorkeeper also saw them and he let out a shout of anger and began to shove his way forward. He was big and strong and pushed the customers aside ruthlessly. Murdoch followed in his wake feeling like a dinghy behind a trawler. When they reached the stage the man grabbed one of the young fellows by the leg and jerked him back to the ground. He gave a yell of pain but was good-naturedly helped to his feet by some of the audience. The second young man, who had the pale skin of a bank clerk, was standing unsteadily in front of the stepladder looking up yearningly at Annie Brogan, who had quickly retreated to her perch. She smiled sweetly and wagged her finger in admonishment, at the same time moving up a rung. Then the manager clambered on the stage, lifted the fellow bodily, and dumped him into the crowd like a sack of coal.

Another round of "Daisy" was in full blast, but Annie held up her hand for silence. The piano player stopped in mid-chord, and there was a gradual quietening as the men blearily started to hush everybody up. When it was quiet enough to make herself heard, she said, "That Daisy could go on forever. She's never spent, is she?"

The innuendo created another wave of laughter. A short sprat of a man in an old-fashioned stovepipe hat called out shrilly, "Hey, Annie, I seen your picture in the *News*. You're famous."

She made a big show of hanging her head. "Reverend Whittaker accused me of indecency. Me of all people... he must not be seeing so good – I wonder why that is?" She waited a moment for them to recover from that one. "All right, you men, here's a riddle for you. I just want to know if you're up tonight. Are you?"

Deafening shouts reverberated through the room and there were a few obscene gestures.

"Ready? What do an American, a rooster, and an old maid have in common?"

"What, Annie, what?" called various of the men.

She looked pert. "An American says, 'Yankee, doodle do.' A rooster says, 'Doodle, doodle do,' and an old maid says, 'Any cock'll do.' No, wait. Wait! I got that wrong, I mean – 'any dude will do.'" Her correction was lost in the laughter. Once again she requested silence.

"Now for my favourite part of the evening… and yours…"

She nodded to the piano player, who began to tinkle the keys softly. She climbed down delicately from the ladder and came back to the edge of the stage, leaning over to speak to the men who were closest. There was a gasp at the sight.

"You, sir. You in the brown cap. What's your name?"

"Archie, miss."

The man was short and wiry with a rather grubby face, as if he never quite got it clean.

"And what's your trade, Charlie?"

He shuffled his feet and looked embarrassed.

"He's a honey man," yelled his companion. There were cries from those beside him who ostentatiously swayed away.

Annie stepped back. "Oh dear! An honest trade if ever I heard of one, but a little too sweet for me I'm afraid."

She surveyed the men pressing in front of her.

"Me! Me!" They were thrusting their hands in the air like boys in a classroom. Annie pointed to one of them who was wearing a beige linen suit that looked as if he'd got it from a secondhand clothes shop on Queen Street. But he had wide shoulders, and even under the too-big coat he looked strong.

"You're a real swell. What do you do?"

He stammered. "I'm a logger, miss."

"My, that's grand. But I don't know if I can ever trust a logging man again."

"Why is that, Annie?" bellowed a tough in the front row.

She pouted. "It was a logging man as ruined my sister."

"Oh no!"

She began to prance back and forth as she told the story.

"My sister is a dear, dear girl, soft-hearted as... sh... well, let's say very soft-hearted. One day this logging man came to her. He was very low." Lots of titters. "His mood, I mean, you naughty men. He told her he was in danger of losing his crib. 'Oh dear,' says she, foolish girl. 'Is there anything I can do to help?' 'There is that,' says Charlie. 'You see, a logging man has to be real handy with his hook. He's got to get those logs unjammed and sometimes they are sooo tight, you just can't get your bill in no how –'" Huge guffaws. Annie acted bewildered. "I don't know what's so funny about that! Let me go on with my story. 'All I need is a little practice,' says he, so my sister, who has too many soft things about her, heart, head, and – well, never mind that. Anyway, she helped that logging man practise all summer with that long, long, long hook of his. But then you know what?"

"What, Annie?" they yelled in unison.

"When winter came *he* was completely cured of his problem

and happily he trotted off to go back to his crib… and now *my sister has a problem*."

Roars of laughter. Rather guiltily, Murdoch found himself smiling too.

Annie held out her hand.

"I hope I can trust you, Charlie. And don't forget I'm wearing my new boots."

She lifted her skirt so they could see. More hollers and hoots. Murdoch was pressed against the stage. The heat was overwhelming and he was sweating. The smell from the bodies jammed against him was rank.

The piano player began to thump out another song.

"I had a sweet little dickie bird…"

The lumberjack clambered on the stage and took Annie clumsily in his arms. They did a waltz around the stage, the logger moving his arm up and down as if he was at the pump. She only tolerated it for two rounds then she let go and led him back to the stairs.

"That was lovely," she said with a grimace, rubbing her arm. "Got the blood flowing. Who's next?"

Murdoch didn't wait. Boldly, he shoved the honey man away from him and vaulted onto the stage. The others shouted disparaging comments. He ignored them and bowed politely to Annie. She curtsied back and Murdoch held up his arms in dance position just as Professor Otranto had taught him.

Annie smiled. "Ha, a dancer I see."

"I sure am," said Murdoch. He didn't add that to date his

only partner had been his teacher, who took the woman's part. His first real dance was coming up next week.

Graciously, Annie stepped up to him. This close he could see how painted her face was, the complexion unnaturally smooth and white, the cheeks and lips rouged. She placed one hand on his shoulder and the other in his. She smiled up at him but it was an impersonal professional smile. He smelled a waft of violet on her breath. As did the good professor, she favoured breath cachous. Her eyes were unnaturally shiny, and as she readied herself he could detect a slight unsteadiness to her stance. *She's as close to being full as you can get without falling over*, he thought.

The piano player started again, the audience joining in.

> *"I had a sweet little dickie bird,*
> *Tweet, tweet tweet, he went..."*

The bobbing red feather pinned in her hair was brushing his nose. They started to waltz, Murdoch trying to pay attention both to her and to his feet. He was counting in his head. One, two, three; one, two, three.

"What do you do when you're not dancing, Charlie?"

He executed a tricky cross-step. She followed easily.

"I'm a police officer. Acting Detective William Murdoch."

The bodice beneath his hand was stiff and unyielding, but even so he felt the sudden tightening of her back. There was a flash of fear across her eyes but the smile replaced it immediately.

"I hope you're not here officially, Mr. Murdoch."

"Tweet, tweet, tweet, he went..."

"As a matter of fact I am. I'd like to have a talk with you."

At that point the harmony between them broke down and he tripped over her feet. She dropped her arms and cried out, making a big to-do of hobbling away.

"Get off the stage, go on, you ox." The men were yelling at him, waving fists; some in good drunken earnest.

The thought flashed through Murdoch's mind that he'd aroused their jealousy with his smooth reverse turn. He stood his ground, although out of the corner of his eye he could see the manager was at the steps ready to move in. He went closer to Annie.

"When?" he asked.

She pirouetted. "After closing time, in my dressing room."

Shirtsleeves was on stage and coming fast towards him. Murdoch jumped down of his own accord.

Annie had called up another dancer, a well-dressed man with dark hair and a sun-tanned, weather-beaten skin. In time to more tweeting they waltzed around the stage and Murdoch was glad to see that the newcomer was no champion. He obviously knew the right steps but he moved so stiffly he could have been a mechanical piece. However, Annie smiled up at him and although Murdoch knew quite well it was all part of the act, he felt a twinge of jealousy.

Leaving them to it, he forced his way through the hot bodies back to the door and finally got outside. Here the air was blessedly cool and he leaned against the wall and wiped his dripping face and neck with his handkerchief. His hand smelled faintly perfumed from Annie's glove and he shifted uncomfortably at the remembered image of all that white, bouncing flesh so close to him.

CHAPTER TWELVE

MURDOCH RETURNED TO THE STATION TO CHECK THE street directory for the Pedlow address and to see what sort of state Crabtree was in. He found the constable in the stable yard. Number-four station possessed two horses, both elderly and reliable, who were used to pull the police ambulance. At the moment, both were in harness. The traces, however, were not hitched to the wagon but to the large frame of George Crabtree. Two of the young constables, Burney and Duncan, were observing, both as alert as seconds in a prize fighter's corner.

Crabtree was stripped down to his singlet and cotton drawers and the reins were wrapped around his thick forearms. He saw Murdoch but was too intent on his task to acknowledge him.

"Ready," he called to Burney.

The constable grasped both bridles, clicked his tongue, and started to lead the horses forward. Crabtree dug into the dirt of the yard with his cleated boots and leaned back. The horses stopped.

"Come on, you. Thut, thut," clucked Burney, and both horses, a bay gelding and a black mare, thrust their muscular shoulders into their collars and took a couple of steps forward. Crabtree yielded some ground but quickly braced himself again and the horses halted.

Again Burney urged them on. Crabtree's body was sharply angled backward, his massive legs pushing into the ground as he tried to hold the pull. The veins in his forehead and neck were so prominent Murdoch was afraid they might burst open. The constable was drenched in sweat and now so low to the ground that his buttocks were inches from touching it. The horses stopped, Captain pawing the ground and tossing his head in bewilderment. For a moment they held, man and beast immobile, but at Burney's shout, the horse moved forward and Crabtree couldn't hold any longer. He started to slide, scrambling desperately to gain a foothold, giving little hops to try to get the dig in. Captain was not to be gainsaid, however, and dragged him on, as Crabtree's boots scraped deep grooves in the dirt.

"Whoa! Whoa!"

Burney halted his charges and they snorted and swished their tails in triumph.

Crabtree collapsed onto his back and Duncan picked up the bucket of water that was in readiness and doused him. Spluttering and shaking his head, the big man sat up. Murdoch went over to him.

"What the hell are you doing?"

"Practising for the pull, sir," gasped the constable.

"Hardly a fair match is it?"

"I don't know, I suppose not."

"For the horses, I mean. Here, let me give you a hand up. Do you want some more water?"

"Thank you, sir."

Murdoch nodded at the other constable who came over with another bucket. Crabtree drank the water.

"Whose idea was this?" Murdoch asked, although he suspected he knew the answer.

"Inspector Brackenreid's. He says the Greeks used to train this way."

"But you've been under the weather. Maybe you're over-doing it."

"I'm not so bad, sir."

He started to wipe himself down with the piece of clean sacking his assistant had handed him.

"Maybe I should be having a look at your teeth," said Murdoch.

"Sir?"

"Never mind. Look, if you're feeling up to it, I'd like you to get over to River Street and help Wiggin with the interviews. The man is as useless as a third tit. I'm going to Jarvis Street. I'll tell you about it while you get dressed."

"I'll just congratulate my competitors," said Crabtree and went over to pet the horses.

"You'd better not stroke the grenadiers' noses when you're up against them," Murdoch called to him. "They might misunderstand."

He was just about to give another tug on the bellpull when the door opened. The young footman stared at him and assumed a faintly supercilious expression.

Murdoch presented his card.

"I wish to speak to Mrs. Pedlow, if you please."

The footman read the card. "Acting Detective, number-four station" was printed neatly beneath Murdoch's name. The servant's superior air dropped away like a thin man's drawers. His alarm was palpable.

"Madam is not at home."

"Is that 'not at home' as in out, or 'not at home' as in doesn't want visitors?"

By the question, Murdoch had violated an unspoken rule of etiquette, but he was in no mood for niceties. The footman was completely flustered.

"She's in but not receiving calls today."

"Maybe she'll make an exception in my case. Will you tell her I'm investigating a very serious police matter and I would appreciate the opportunity to speak to her."

The footman stared at him. Murdoch thought his behaviour was odd but people often reacted like that when they knew who he was. A spotless conscience seemed a rarity.

"Will you step inside, Mr., er, Murdoch? I will see if Mrs. Pedlow is available."

"And what's your name, young man? I might need to talk to you as well."

Murdoch was only partly bluffing. He might indeed have to question the servants. It depended on what Mrs. Pedlow had to say for herself. The footman looked even more ill at ease.

"I'm John Meredith. But what would you want to talk to me about?"

"I don't exactly know until I've had my chat with Mrs. Pedlow."

Suddenly the footman's face brightened with relief, like a condemned man who'd got a pardon. "I'll go fetch her."

Forgetting all his training, he backed away awkwardly, leaving Murdoch to enter and close the doors behind him.

The entrance hall where he stood was sumptuous and felt vaguely ecclesiastical. A mahogany staircase, the balustrade elaborately carved, swept off to the side. A crystal chandelier, with what looked like electric light, tinkled softly in the sweep of air. Glancing around, he saw why he had been put in mind of a church. To his right was a tall stained-glass window depicting St. George slaying the dragon. The saint was young and muscular in his white armour with the red cross, the dragon green and ferocious. In front of the window was a three-legged table on top of which was an embossed silver salver for visitor's cards. Curious, Murdoch stirred them with his finger. What was it again? When he was a young man he had studied all the etiquette books he could find, conscious of his own ignorant beginnings. However, maturity and Liza had tempered that anxiety. She had known much more about how to apply the necessary oils to the wheels of polite society. Not that their calls and visits to friends were formal. The opposite really. More likely to be outings to the lake or a ferry ride to the island than a stiff conversation in the drawing room.

He picked up one of the cards. He remembered now. Mrs. Simon Curzon had turned down the right end of her card, which meant she had come in person. He'd seen her name often in the newspaper, organizing some event or other for the Women's Historical Society. Mrs. Laura Spurr and her daughter Miss Georgiana Spurr had both left cards, folded in the middle to indicate they were calling on all the family. Miss Spurr was an artist. Portraits of Toronto society, if he remembered correctly. Perhaps Mrs. Pedlow was a customer.

His boots had rung out on the hard surface of the hall floor and looking down he saw it was of pink and grey Italian marble. Perfect for dancing. He almost felt like doing a quick jig right on the spot.

However, Meredith came down the stairs and forestalled him. "Mrs. Pedlow will be most happy to receive you," said the footman. "Please to wait in here and she will be with you right away."

He ushered the detective through the tapestry portieres into the drawing room.

Murdoch removed his hat but didn't sit down. He'd started to perspire, partly from a nervousness he despised in himself, and partly because the room was uncomfortably warm. A completely unnecessary fire had been lit in the hearth.

Consistent with the grand entrance hall, this room was spacious and luxurious. The walls were panelled in white wood with an ebony trim, and above the wainscot was flowered paper of crimson flock. More flowers, yellow and red roses, patterned the hunter green carpet, which was thick enough for a dog to bury a bone in. Or a pauper his pittance.

He walked over to the fireplace, which dominated the far wall. An oil painting in a massive gilt-edged oak frame was hung above the mantel. Murdoch recognized the portrait of Judge Pedlow in his robe of office. It must have been painted fairly recently, because his honour looked older than Murdoch remembered. However, the artist, either through inadequate skills or fundamental honesty, had not softened the harsh line of the jaw or the tightness of the mouth. Pedlow looked just as mean-spirited and severe as he remembered.

Murdoch fingered the calling card he'd put in his pocket. You never knew, maybe a little dirt from this case would rub off on his lordship.

There was a large mechanical piece on a marble stand next to the hearth, and curious, he turned to have a look at it. He'd heard about these things but had never actually seen one before. Inside a glass cover, two monkeys dressed in blue and red satin were seated at a table in a saloon surrounded by mirrors. One held a cigar, the other an ornate box. Presumably when the piece was wound up the monkeys moved and music played.

He was saved from temptation by the entrance of Mrs. Pedlow.

"Mr. Murdoch, I'm sorry if I kept you waiting."

The woman greeting him was younger than he expected, slight of build, with light brown hair curled around her forehead and cheeks in the latest style. The startling thing about her, however, was the lumpy wine-coloured birthmark that covered her right cheek. Her voice was rather haughty, an impression heightened by the slight upward turn of the corner of her lip.

She indicated one of the chairs.

"Do sit down."

She took a chair across from him and at an angle. He could see she was adept at seating herself in such a way the disfigurement of her right cheek was partly obscured. She was handsomely dressed in a cream-coloured satin gown trimmed at the bodice and skirt with narrow bands of purple. The sleeves were full and puffed at the top, which also masked the naevus. There was as much lace at the neck and cuffs of the sleeves as his bishop wore on holy days. If this was how she dressed when she wasn't receiving, he wondered what her gown was like when she was "at home".

"May I offer some refreshment?"

"No, thank you, ma'am."

Hands clasped tightly in her lap, she waited for him to begin.

"I'm conducting a police investigation, ma'am, and I wonder if I could ask you a few questions?"

"Of course."

"Would you happen to know, or have you ever heard of, a woman named Dolly Shaw? She lived at River Street at the corner of Wilton."

Maud Pedlow managed to indicate slightly offended surprise. "Not at all, Mr. Murdoch. I cannot imagine why I should."

He took the calling card from his pocket.

"This is yours, I presume, Mrs. Pedlow?"

She took it from him as gingerly as if it would crumble at the touch. "Yes, it is mine. Why do you have it?"

"I found it in Mrs. Shaw's desk."

"How strange. I assure you it is not because I paid her a call."

Mrs. Pedlow spoke as if the notion was utterly absurd, knowing Dolly Shaw to be riff-raff. However, he couldn't make too much of that. Most people of Maud's standing would make the same assumption. The better class of people wouldn't be involved with the police in life or death.

"Is something the matter that you are enquiring? Does it have anything to do with Mr. Pedlow's being a judge?"

"I don't know about that, ma'am. But yes, I'd say there is something very much the matter. The woman was murdered."

Maud jumped at his emphatic tone and her hand flew to her damaged cheek. He waited for questions but none came, and once again he was at a loss to know if this was typical behaviour in polite society or because she already knew the answers.

"I'm sorry, Mr. Murdoch. What you've told me is shocking but I don't see I can be of any help. One of my cards must have come into her possession by chance."

"The dead woman's daughter takes in laundry to wash. Could there be a connection that way? Her name is Lily."

"I don't know her either but it sounds likely she could have picked up my card from somebody's house. One of her customers. Perhaps she was intending to approach me for work."

Maybe, but he wasn't prepared to give up yet. He hesitated, searching for the appropriate words. "I have been told that Mrs. Shaw was once a midwife and that she served women in all aspects of their pregnancy."

She stared at him. "I see. Are you suggesting one of my servants might be, er, involved?"

He shrugged.

"It is highly unlikely," she continued quickly. "None of them have given any, er, sign. His lordship has very high standards of behaviour, thinking that any immorality in his own household would reflect adversely on his position and example."

"And rightly so, ma'am."

He had to admit she'd shifted the focus most adroitly but whether that was from cunning or the arrogance of her class, he couldn't tell. He was aware this woman was uncomfortable and nervous and did not want to appear so.

"Would anybody have received a letter from Mrs. Shaw?"

"No."

"You are speaking for yourself, I assume, ma'am?"

"Yes, of course, but the servants do not receive mail. Burns would tell me if they did."

"Do you know a Miss Brogan, ma'am? Miss Annie Brogan. She is an entertainer. An internationally acclaimed chanteuse."

"No, I don't." She paused and her eyes met his. "Is she implicated?"

"I've not come to any conclusions yet, ma'am. I'm just following up every possibility."

There was a silence and he waited until her attention returned to him.

"I'm sorry I couldn't help more. Now if you will excuse me... we will be serving tea shortly. My husband likes us to be punctual."

"I would like to speak with your servants, if you please, ma'am."

"Is that necessary? How could they know any more than I?"

"As you have implied, ma'am, a woman like Dolly Shaw would be more likely to associate with your servants than with yourself."

"I do think you are carrying your zeal too far, Mr. Murdoch. I don't want the servants disturbed. I have two young maids. Who knows if this will throw them into hysterics."

"I shall be most tactful and I must remind you I am investigating the most serious of crimes. A woman murdered in her own home. Come now, Mrs. Pedlow. You are married to a judge. You must value the law, surely? Besides, I doubt your maids will take a conniption over some poor old woman they've never heard of. And if they are as pure as you say, the other thing will not trouble them. I'm afraid I have to insist, ma'am."

Before she could answer, there was a soft tap at the door and the butler entered.

"Shall I prepare tea soon, madam?"

"Thank you, Burns."

Murdoch got to his feet. "Your permission, ma'am?"

Not looking at him, she said, "I don't seem to have much choice in the matter." She turned to the butler. "Burns, will you take Mr. Murdoch to the kitchen and fetch in the servants. He is a detective. He would like to talk to everybody."

The butler's eyes flickered over to Murdoch. He tried to act as impassively as if she'd been talking about introducing the new rector but he didn't quite succeed.

"What does it have to do with us here, if I may be so bold as to ask, madam?"

"I'll explain all that," said Murdoch.

"You'd better start with Susan," said Mrs. Pedlow.

"Where is she?"

"She's turning out the upper bedrooms, madam."

"Go and get her will you? I'll direct Mr. Murdoch to the kitchen."

Burns left, his curiosity hovering on the air like a smell. Maud turned back to Murdoch.

"Did you say that there is a young woman involved? A singer?"

"I don't yet know how involved she is, but we have a witness who claims Miss Brogan entered Mrs. Shaw's house late on the night of the murder."

"A witness?"

"A neighbour. He suffers from insomnia and he was at his window."

Mrs. Pedlow stood up and walked over to the mechanical piece. Her back was to Murdoch. "I forgot. That is, I didn't realize until this moment, but there was a young woman who came here. Now that I recall she said her name was Brogan. That was the name you mentioned, was it not?"

"Yes, ma'am. Annie Brogan."

"My footman has apparently seduced her sister and got her with child, so she came here to confront him."

Murdoch hadn't expected this.

"What day was this, ma'am?"

"The Friday last."

"Did you talk with her yourself?"

"Very briefly. My ward and I were on our way out when we encountered her and her sister on the doorstep."

"And you hadn't seen her before?"

"She was a total stranger to me."

"Have you seen her since?"

Maud started to wind up the mechanical apparatus. "Now that you ask, she did in fact return on Saturday. I almost forgot. She wanted me to help her. See that Meredith did the right thing. Of course I will do my best. But perhaps this isn't the woman you are seeking."

"Did she mention where she worked? Where she did her singing?"

"No, she didn't. As I said it was the briefest of visits. We merely discussed what to do about her sister's situation."

Murdoch nodded. "I'll talk to the servants now then, ma'am. If you'll be so good as to show me the way."

The monkeys started to move. The cigar smoker raised the cigar to his lips, the other monkey opened his box and took out dice. A lively piece of music accompanied this action. Murdoch was glad he'd seen the thing in operation, and he looked forward to telling Arthur and Beatrice all about it.

The kitchen was filled with the necessities for maintaining a rich household. There were three tall pine cupboards along the far wall, and an enormous gleaming Sunshine range squatted opposite. Iron pots and pans hung from a grid suspended from the ceiling. There was even an icebox tucked in the corner. A short, grey-haired woman was chopping vegetables at a table by the stove. At first Murdoch thought she was bald, but closer he saw that she had pulled back her grey hair so tightly from her pinched face, that the shape of her skull was prominent. Burns introduced her as his wife, Hannah.

"Detective Murdoch is here to investigate a murder, my dear." The woman looked up at Murdoch, her eyes streaming with tears. For a split second he didn't know what on earth was the matter, then the corresponding sting in his own eyes made him realize she was chopping onions. She sniffed hard and wiped her runny nose with the back of her hand. Burns went on to summarize what Murdoch had told him. Hannah was unimpressed. No, she had never heard of Dolly Shaw or Annie Brogan. She kept to herself, thank you, like any Christian woman should. They did their own washing, even had an electric tumbler, she said with as much pride as if it were her own. As to the story about Meredith and Annie Brogan's visit, it didn't surprise her at all. Actresses were no better than women of the night as far as she was concerned. Murdoch didn't bother to correct her that it was Annie's sister who was in the family way. Mrs. Burns had hardly got all this off her chest, which was as tight as her hair, when there was a high-pitched whistling sound from the direction of the door. Burns went over immediately and Murdoch saw a row of small bells, each with a label above them. To one side was a curved tube. The butler pulled off a little lid and put his ear against the end of the tube. He listened for a few moments then he shouted into the opening.

"Yes, madam, right away."

His wife looked up at him questioningly.

"She wants the carriage brought out. Says she has to go on an errand."

"That's awkward. Taylor's mending the tack and he's got to get his lordship from the courthouse by four. She specifically said she wouldn't want the carriage today."

Burns shrugged. "No use telling me that. She's changed her mind and she's in a hurry." He pushed a button that presumably connected with the stable. "I thought I'd set Mr. Murdoch up for his investigations in my pantry. Out of everybody's way." He meant out of her way and Murdoch was grateful. He wouldn't have liked to be making his enquiries under the cold stare of Mrs. Burns. The butler had ranked Murdoch to his own satisfaction and was much friendlier. He ushered Murdoch over to a small room off the kitchen. It was just big enough to hold a desk and two chairs, one behind and one in front. There was a glass-fronted lawyer's cabinet along the wall stocked with bound registers. Burns seemed to be a tidy man. While he went to fetch the first of the servants, Murdoch took out his notebook and placed it in the middle of the desk. All ready for business.

The questioning took almost two hours, and the most interesting interviews were the ones with John Meredith and Maud's personal maid, Louise Kenny.

Initially, the young footman obviously thought he was going to be charged with seduction but when Murdoch made it clear he wasn't interested in Meredith's love life, he relaxed. No, he didn't know any Dolly Shaw but he did admit to knowing Annie Brogan, in a manner of speaking. With more bravado than shame he narrated to Murdoch his encounter with the two sisters on Friday.

"You could have tipped my arse with a goose feather when they appeared like that. I mean I didn't know Millie had got one on the go. Terrible shock it was and the three of us dithering on the doorstep like tarts at the church door. Then out comes the mistress." He paused and eyed Murdoch shrewdly. "That was very odd, I tell you. You'd think Annie and her knew each other but weren't having on they did. But God knows where they would have met, given who she is."

"I take it Annie Brogan is who you are referring to?"

"'Course. Anyways, she is a bold one, that doxie. Before you could wink, she'd asked mistress if she could take Miss Sarah down to the opera house. Show her around! And the missus said yes, sweet as you please. Come for tea and we'll discuss it, like she was a proper person."

Murdoch frowned. That wasn't what Mrs. Pedlow had told him at all.

"Did you see Miss Brogan when she came on Saturday?"

"Not really. She and missus met in the gazebo out in the garden." He leaned forward and placed his forefinger on his nose. "I was polishing the brasses at the time but I tell you man to man, I considered it in my best interests to keep an eye on the proceedings so I peeked out the window. I tell you they were thick as flies on offal."

"How long did she stay?"

"Quite a long time."

"How long? Twenty minutes? An hour?"

"A good forty minutes, I'd say."

So much for Maud's "briefest of visits", or maybe she had a different concept of time from most people.

He changed tack. "Who fetches the mail?"

"I do."

Murdoch took out the letter he'd found in Dolly's desk. He folded the bottom so Meredith could see only the first line of writing. No sense in getting rumours started.

"Ever see a letter with this handwriting?"

Meredith shook his head. "Never. Most of what comes is legal sort of things for his honour."

"You're certain?"

"Sure as houses. I'd remember."

Like most servants, Meredith took a lively interest in his employer's affairs.

"Has anything been hand-delivered?"

"When?"

"I don't know," Murdoch replied irritably. "Anytime. Recently. Last year."

"Not that I recall. I've been here for five years. I see everybody that comes to the door. If they're trades and they brought anything, Mrs. Burns would let me know. I take it in to madam or his honour. I'd remember. I've got a good memory."

"Too bad you didn't remember you already had a fiancée when you seduced Mildred Brogan."

The footman was unabashed. Murdoch could read his mind. He thought the detective was speaking out of jealousy. "She was willing. Eager, if you want to know."

"I don't. So what are you going to do? The decent thing?"

Meredith looked sullen. "Can't, can I? Ellen's father has a nice dry goods store on King Street, and the idea is that he'll take me into the business when we're married. How can I pass that up?"

"How indeed? Maybe you should have thought of that before you put one in the oven."

That deflated Meredith sufficiently to give Murdoch some satisfaction and he dismissed him.

The scullery maid and the general servant were sisters, Mary and Susan Davis. Murdoch interviewed them together to guard against hysterics. However, they were two sturdy young women, both with the fresh colour and firm flesh of country girls. The older one, Susan, expressed sympathy for the dead woman, which nobody else had done. They knew nothing, had not met her or Lily or seen the Brogans when they arrived. Monday was washing day but it had rained so they'd had to do the laundry on Friday, and both of them had spent the entire day in the downstairs scullery. The only nervousness they exhibited was that they might be blamed for something, they knew not what. Mr. Burns was swift with his deductions, said Susan, and they were trying to support a large tribe of brothers and sisters up in Bradford. They couldn't afford to be docked any wages. Murdoch then told them bluntly about Dolly's illegal services but they weren't too shocked about that either. Susan laughed.

"You don't have to worry about none of the servants getting into trouble in this household. His lordship probably knows when we use the privy let alone anything else. Nobody is allowed a follower or you get sacked. We should have been nuns. Have a better time."

Murdoch didn't like her last comment but he knew she didn't mean real harm. He showed them the letter but they said they never saw the mail. The trades that came to the back door were handled by Mrs. Burns. Murdoch thanked them and they went off to turn out another bedroom.

The next interview was with Maud's personal maid, Louise Kenny.

She entered in a miasma of patchouli oil which she must have applied recently. A tall woman, rather big-boned, she was definitely not suited to fluttering. How ever, she had brought a dainty tortoiseshell fan with her and she snapped it open and closed at regular intervals. She was wearing a deep blue satin waist with a high sulphur-yellow collar and matching cuffs. Her skirt was rustle taffeta of a turquoise tint.

She was eager to help but had nothing to contribute, although she tried hard. Every time Murdoch asked a question she opened her fan, waved it vigorously while she gave the matter the serious consideration it deserved, then snapped it shut to answer. Unfortunately, she did not know anybody by the name of Dolly Shaw, although she had known a Doris Shawcross who had passed away three years ago. No, she had no acquaintance with Annie Brogan and was not aware she had visited Mrs. Pedlow on Saturday afternoon. Madam had not mentioned she was having callers. She, Miss Kenny, had been upstairs tending to the mistress's gowns the whole day.

"She only buys the absolute best, imported for the most part from Paris, France, so we do have to take very good care of them."

Murdoch had the feeling that Miss Kenny wanted to tell him something but didn't know how to get started. He decided to let loose a lure and see what happened.

"If I may say so, Miss Kenny, I feel sorry for the lady. She would be a handsome woman except for the..."

He waved his hand over his cheek.

Miss Kenny sighed. "That is so true. And money won't compensate, will it?"

He shook his head soberly. "Fortunately she has her little ward. Children don't notice these defects, do they?"

"Not when they're young, but the child remarked on it the other day. 'Can you scrub it off, Auntie?' she asks her. I could see that the mistress was upset, but she didn't give the child any reprimand as she probably should have. But then she never does. It's murder for the nursemaids, I can tell you. They can't offer one correction or scold to that girl or they'll be sacked on the spot. Fortunately for all of us, Miss Sarah is a sweet-natured child and not difficult to manage."

"How long have you been in Mrs. Pedlow's employ?"

"Seven and one half years. She had just returned from England. The poor little orphan was barely six months old at the time." She tilted her head, speaking confidentially. "Her own mother was Mrs. Pedlow's cousin and died in childbirth. The husband had already been taken off by the influenza. What a tragedy. His lordship wasn't overjoyed at the idea of a ward, but he couldn't do much with the infant on the doorstep, could he?"

Murdoch bent towards her. He could see that Miss Kenny used face powder on her rather broad nose, and Nature could not have tinted her cheeks with such an even blush.

"Between you and me, Miss Kenny, I am sometimes at a loss as to why certain folks ever get married. His lordship and Mrs. Pedlow seem as different as chalk and cheese."

She smiled. "How right you are. But perhaps for her..." Like Murdoch she fluttered her hand in the area of her right cheek. "I would never do that, myself. My mother always said I was as particular as a princess because I turned down suitor after suitor."

"Perhaps that was not such a good comparison. The royal princesses don't really have much choice in husbands, do they?"

She looked at him, trying to determine the intent of his comment. "I suppose not."

He had meant nothing by the remark but he had hurt her feelings in some obscure way he couldn't quite fathom. "As you were saying, Miss Kenny?"

"Just that I was a foolish girl and thought youth would last forever. I am much mellowed now, having seen too much of life to expect perfection. Even Lord Byron had his faults."

Murdoch wasn't entirely sure who the imperfect lord was but there was no mistaking the wistfulness in Miss Kenny's voice. She was in the market for a husband. He sat back abruptly in his chair. She was affected, plain, and in his opinion had a terrible taste in clothes, but there was something about her that moved him. Perhaps because he could sense her aching loneliness and that he understood.

He considered briefly, then he said, "I have no desire to

place you in an untenable position but I am interested in your opinion. I tell you frankly that your mistress has not been absolutely candid with me. Not big things as far as I can determine, but me being the suspicious man that I am, I'm always bothered if I'm handed even small lies."

"Such as?"

"The young woman I mentioned, Annie Brogan, came here to call on Saturday and stayed for almost an hour. Mrs. Pedlow at first denied all knowledge of the girl but when it became apparent I would find out, she pretended it was the most brief and casual of visits. John Meredith felt there was something odd about the meeting between Miss Brogan and Mrs. Pedlow. He wondered if they had met before."

"I'd swear not while I've been in Mrs. Pedlow's service."

"She strikes me as a highly strung woman. What is your impression, Miss Kenny? Is there anything distressing her?"

Murdoch knew he was taking a risk, that Louise Kenny might be affronted in her loyalties to her mistress. She stared at him for a moment then put the fan at rest in her lap.

"In my opinion she was upset when Mr. Henry Pedlow, his lordship's nephew, showed up from India. Nobody expected him. In he waltzes as if he'd just come back from a swim at Sunnyside. I don't think she can abide the man. She's so flustered and jumpy whenever he's around."

"Is that all that's bothering her? An unwelcome visitor?"

"Nothing else untoward has happened."

"Is her marriage happy would you say?"

"As much as possible –"

"Given her husband is Walter Pedlow?"

She nodded, snapping the fan open and wafting it vigorously.

"Miss Kenny, might I ask you for a favour?"

"If I can."

He lowered his voice and explained what he wanted.

CHAPTER THIRTEEN

ANNIE'S DRESSING ROOM WAS EVEN SMALLER THAN Murdoch's own cubicle at the station. There was room for a shabby dresser, an extra cane chair, and a sagging pouf. Across one corner was strung a peacock blue chenille curtain. The tiny space was bare of clutter but from the rather lumpy hang of the curtain, Murdoch had the sense that things had been hastily stuffed away for his benefit. Annie hadn't changed out of her stage costume but she'd covered her bosom with a grey, honeycomb shawl which she might have borrowed from her granny. She'd also removed the makeup from her face. Except for the spangled scarlet skirt that showed beneath the shawl, she looked neat and proper. She did not want to give offence.

"Please sit down. That chair isn't as fragile as it looks."

He took the cane chair, which swayed and creaked alarmingly.

"What can I do for you, Mr., er, I'm sorry but I've forgotten your name already."

"It isn't Charlie."

She shrugged. "There's too many of them to remember. Charlie suits."

"My name's Murdoch. William Murdoch."

"And you're a police officer?"

She wrinkled her forehead prettily as if the idea of police officers was bewildering.

"That's right. Acting detective, number-four station."

She turned to face the dresser mirror and absentmindedly smoothed her hair back into one of her combs. She continued to look at his reflection and he was forced to address her the same way.

"I'm conducting an investigation and I thought you might be able to help."

"If I can, of course. I like to be of help."

Somehow she managed to make it sound lascivious.

"Did you by any chance know a Mrs. Shaw? Dolly Shaw? She lived on River Street."

Annie's eyes narrowed and she became still. "Never heard of her. Why d'you ask?"

"She's dead."

She swivelled around and met his gaze properly.

"What! When'd that happen?"

"She was found stone cold dead in her own parlour last Friday morning."

Annie stared at him and gave a little laugh.

"Come on, Mr. Murdoch, spit it out. What happened, for God's sake?"

"The coroner says she was suffocated."

"Suffocated how?"

"I'm not at liberty to disclose the method of death, ma'am. But I can tell you it was not from natural causes."

She picked up the ostrich feather fan from the dresser and began to fan herself. She did it more gracefully than Miss Louise Kenny but for similar reasons.

"If it wasn't natural then it was unnatural. In my book, that means somebody done her in. Is that right?"

"It is."

"Why've you come here? What's it to do with me?"

"One of the neighbours was looking out his window late on Thursday night. Fellow couldn't sleep. He says he saw a young woman enter Mrs. Shaw's house. At about a quarter past midnight. He says that woman was you, Miss Brogan."

"That's a load of horse plop. I told you I've never heard of the woman. He's got the wrong person. How can you believe some old gasper who's sitting there pulling on his dick 'til he goes blind?"

"Stow the language. Mr. Golding says he recognized you because you'd had a little encounter the week previous.

When you were coming into the Derby here. He was outside preaching Temperance."

"What sort of frigging encounter?"

"He says you knocked over a Miss Yielding who was his assistant."

Annie grinned suddenly. "I remember the man now. Ugly as a devil's dick. Got all these lumps all over him. That's the one, isn't it?"

Murdoch nodded.

"He's trying to get back at me. I didn't push the stupid hummer over. She slipped. She wanted to stick a tract up my nose and I was startled. It wasn't my fault. He's making up this story to get me in trouble, the prick."

"I asked you to watch your language."

She sneered. "Sorry, I didn't realize I was in the presence of unstained youth."

"Can you prove where you were then? Last Thursday night, say from ten to morning."

"I was at home in my bed, where else? Fast asleep."

"Do you live by yourself?"

"'Course not. My sister Millie and me doss down on Mill Street."

"She could confirm that you were at home?"

"Of course. But believe me, that's where I was, not murdering some bint on River Street."

"Do you know anybody by the name of Pedlow, Mrs. Maud Pedlow?"

"No."

"That's odd. She says you went to visit her on Saturday."

"I did?"

"You did. And don't tell me she's lying because the footman also says you were there."

"Does he now? Well maybe he's having it off with his missus and agrees to anything she says."

Murdoch felt like shaking her. "Listen to me, Annie Brogan. All I have to do is take you to the station and bring them in. Of course they'll identify you. Stop giving me a lot of queer."

"It's not me, it's you. You come in here, throwing your weight around. I visit lots of people. Why are you asking me about this particular bint?"

He almost laughed. "All right, fair enough. When I was examining Dolly Shaw's desk I found Mrs. Pedlow's calling card. I went to question said lady just in case and discovered you'd been there previously. I thought it was quite a coincidence seeing as how you seemed to be connected with the murder victim."

"Friggin' hell," Annie exploded. "I just told you that's horse plop, dog pure, bull patties, whatever you want to call it. Or shall I just say shit? That is shit."

"Cut it out, I said. You asked me why I wanted to know about you and Mrs. Pedlow and I'm telling you."

Annie, her eyes angry and fearful, turned back to her mirror and began to rub large patches of rouge on her cheeks.

"So did she know anything, the judge's wife?"

"Just like you, she'd never heard of Dolly Shaw."

Suddenly Annie snapped her fingers and in a totally unconvincing display she said, "I know who you mean now. I was getting confused. Didn't really know her name. Pedlow, that's it. I did go to see her. It's true. Saturday."

"Why did you do that?"

"Do I have to tell you?"

"I've already said I'm investigating a murder case. Do you want me to issue a subpoena?"

She continued to paint her face. Dipping her little finger into a small pot on the dresser, she applied a blue paste to her eyelids.

"I've had enough of those things, thank you. It's just that it doesn't involve me so much as my sister, and she has a right to privacy, doesn't she?"

"I know about her pregnancy if that's what you're referring to."

She squeezed some black paint out of a tube on to a dainty brush. "Meredith told you?"

Murdoch nodded.

"The man got his tool into my sister and she's got one on the go. He says he can't marry her, that he's betrothed to some other poor woman. I've always looked after my sister and I thought the mistress of the house might help us to make Mr. Merry Dick see the error of his ways."

"And will she?"

"She says so. Very kind lady. She's going to look out for a position for both of them. After they're married."

"Meredith thought you and Mrs. Pedlow were very chummy."

"Did he?" She applied a thick black line on her lower lid and began to draw in lashes. "Well we're all sisters under the skin, aren't we. Like I said, she's a kind lady. She sympathized with my situation. Talking about men draws women closer. We got along like bees on shit."

"Dolly Shaw was in possession of some herbs that will bring on a miscarriage."

His attempt to unsettle her didn't work.

She was reddening her full lips now, in complete control.

"As far as I'm concerned, it's a good thing somebody will help women when they need it. Prevents a lot of misery."

"Maybe you went to River Street to get something to bring on your sister."

"I already told you I didn't." She tapped on his notebook with a long fingernail. "You'd better write it down. You keep forgetting."

He was getting nowhere and he was so exasperated he knew it could affect his judgement. It was not out of the question that Golding had made up the story, but he hadn't seemed like a vindictive man. However, he'd already made one assumption that was wrong. He didn't want to make the same mistake with Annie Brogan.

"Give me your exact address, I'm going to have to speak to your sister."

There was a sharp rap on the door.

"Visitor, Annie!"

"Just a minute."

"I live at number two-forty-seven, Mill Street, right across from the distillery. Nice down there, smells good. Will you leave now? You've got your answer. People who come here aren't that partial to police officers. I don't want to frighten them off, do I?"

Murdoch entered the information in his notebook, picked up his hat, and squeezed past Annie to the door. As he did so, she untied the demure shawl, letting it fall so that her breasts swelled into view. She watched for his reaction in the mirror and smiled in satisfaction when she caught the unavoidable glance.

When he stepped out into the hall, a young man was leaning against the wall, waiting. It was the long-haired dandy who had got up to dance with Annie earlier. He did not respond to Murdoch's acknowledgement. Morose fellow. He and Annie Brogan deserved each other.

He went directly to Mill Street and, as he expected, a frightened Millie Brogan confirmed her sister's alibi. He could get no other information and she cried so easily and so constantly, he left as soon as he could.

It was a fair hike from there back up to Jarvis Street and Louise Kenny was already waiting for him outside Saltley. As soon as she saw him approaching she hurried towards him. She had changed her clothes and at first he didn't know why she looked so odd. Then he realized she was wearing a dress that was more suitable for winter and seemed far too small for her.

It was a woollen walking costume, dark green with wide lapels of brown satin and an abundance of gold trimming along the seams. Her wrists protruded out of the sleeves, her yellow kid gloves didn't suit.

She indicated the house behind her. "Can we walk a little?" She was quite excited and, far from feeling guilty, she was obviously enjoying the role of informer. He offered her his arm and sedately they proceeded up Jarvis Street. Her hat was so wide and loaded with artificial fruit and flowers that he wondered she could even hold her head up. It meant he had to keep his distance or risk blinding from one of the stems.

"Mr. Murdoch, I only can spare twenty minutes at the most."

"Mrs. Pedlow is back then?"

"Yes. She was out for about an hour."

"And?"

"I asked Taylor as you requested and he said she went to the Avonmore Hotel. That's where Henry Pedlow is staying."

"You thought Mrs. Pedlow didn't like her nephew but she seems most eager to see him, upsetting everybody's plans like that."

"Most peculiar, isn't it? Taylor was ticked off because the horse has been a bit lame and Mrs. Pedlow insisted on going at a canter all the way to the hotel. As if they were going to a fire."

Or from one, thought Murdoch.

"She has been quite out of sorts since she returned. She has requested dinner to be served in her own sitting room and she doesn't even want to be with Miss Sarah."

"Did Taylor know why? What happened?"

Louise frowned. "Taylor is interested only in horses, Mr. Murdoch. Or whether or not the carriage has a squeak. His own mother could be sitting in front of him in a state of suicidal melancholy and he wouldn't notice."

Her voice was sharp and Murdoch wondered if the oblivious coachman had previously stirred Miss Kenny's affections.

"Is she in some sort of trouble?" she asked.

"Frankly, I don't know."

"I must say, I hope not. She is not a warm woman but she can be generous. She gives me her gowns when she no longer needs them."

"Is that one of them?"

"Yes. I had to alter it a little but it is imported from New York, in America, and there is not another one like it in all of Toronto."

"Most becoming, if I may say so, Miss Kenny."

She flushed and looked so happy he felt like a rat. He was acting as self-serving as any masher and it wasn't fair.

"One more thing, Miss Kenny." He took the calling card out of his pocket and showed it to her. "This does belong to Mrs. Pedlow, does it not?"

She studied the card briefly. "In a manner of speaking. She has much more fashionable cards now. Narrower, with a more flowing print. I haven't seen this style before."

"Thank you. You have been invaluable."

It was time to turn around and take her back. At the gate, she offered him her hand to shake.

"If I can be of further assistance, please don't hesitate to contact me. I will be most discreet."

Her expression was so wistful, he almost wished he had another task for her.

CHAPTER FOURTEEN

LILY LAY WATCHING THE SKY THROUGH THE TREES. SHE had been lying like this for a long time, until the stars disappeared and the branches came into relief against the coming dawn. When she was in jail, she had spent most of her time watching the window. All she could see was a patch of sky, all that happened was the changing of the light. She concentrated on that until she fell into a trance-like state that was warm and safe. She would go there and not stir until the matron shook her roughly awake and indicated it was time for the next meal. Everybody treated her as if she were simple, even the other inmates. Some of them truly were simple and others were insane. Most of them, however, were poor women who committed crimes out of desperate need. A few of these had made a living as prostitutes and they were treated the worst.

Lily knew what she had done was so bad even these outcasts shunned her, and in the lonely five years of her imprisonment she made friends with no one.

Stiffly, she crawled out of the den. Her side ached from the hard ground and as best as she could she stretched underneath the branches of the willow. The river was fretting against the fallen tree as if it wanted to move it out of the way. Lily reached over, scooped up some water, and poured it over her forehead. And again, and once again. When she was a young girl, she had watched a christening in the village church. The priest had made those gestures over the newborn infant. The baby hadn't cried at all, a good sign, and the parents and grandparents gathered around the font seemed joyous. The baby was bathed in their delight and welcome.

When Lily had taken the other baby, she had baptized it with water in the same way, needing to participate in such a ritual.

One of the girls in her mother's care had given birth to a deformed child. It had a gaping maw where a mouth should be and the tiny fingers were webbed together. The girl, horrified, had thrust it away from her, refused to tend to it, and Lily understood that the child would be left to die. The next night, driven to desperation by the infant's weakening cries, she took the poor creature out of its cradle and escaped to the woods. She knew of a crude shelter, and after placing the baby on a bed of moss and grass, she went in search of food. She managed to get milk from the Parkers' cow, which was standing in a nearby field, and painstakingly she dribbled the rich cream into the infant's mouth. At first the baby, a girl child, seemed happier, nestling into her bosom, sucking as best as she could at the twist of clean linen that Lily had fashioned for a teat. However, she soon became weaker and weaker and was unable to retain the smallest amount of nourishment, finally not even water from the stream. She didn't cry or fuss, simply lay quietly in Lily's arms. She died there on the fourth day. Lily saw the moment of death, saw the frail breath stop, but she held the tiny body close until the child was grey and cold.

That is how the policeman and the searchers found her. In the doorway of a falling-down hut in the middle of the woods. She refused to give up the dead infant until, in exasperation, the officer clouted her across the head and she had to let go.

The father of the young woman who had given birth was a prosperous merchant and he was only too happy to divert his wrath from his daughter to Lily. The coroner later said that the baby had been born with incomplete digestive organs and would not have lived. Perhaps Lily even prolonged its life. Nevertheless the law, urged on by the righteous anger of the man of commerce, would not tolerate what was essentially kidnapping. Lily was summarily charged and sentenced to five years' imprisonment. "You are lucky to get such a lenient sentence," said her mother and Lily understood her.

The scandal eventually drove them out of the village. Dolly drew fewer and fewer clients and, embittered, made matters worse by drinking too much. She finally moved to Toronto and changed her name. Lily left prison after four years and six months but she was no longer so pliable as she had been. When Dolly's brutality got too much, she fought back like a baited bear until even Dolly kept a wide berth.

Millie Brogan slipped out of bed, rushed into the adjoining kitchen, and vomited yellow bile into the slop pail. And again. There was nothing in her stomach and the vomiting gave no relief. Trying not to groan as she didn't want to wake Annie, she got to her feet. She ladled some water into the bowl and rinsed out her mouth. As she did so, she caught sight of her own reflection in the fly-speckled mirror over the sink. Millie was not vain. You couldn't grow up with a sister like Annie and consider yourself pretty. But she was only twenty-three years old and she looked forty. Her eyes were dark and hollowed and her hair was stringy and dull about her face. She could have wept at the sight. Annie's cruel words had stuck in her head. "Why any man would want to have a bit off with you, I don't know."

Is that all it had been? A bit on the side? When she had first seen John at the church meeting, he'd seemed so handsome with his brown eyes that bespoke intelligence and energy, his mouth that seemed to want to turn up at the corners in merriment. He wasn't tall, but straight-backed and smart in his black serge suit and dashing striped four-in-hand. She was sitting across the aisle from him, and catching her eye, he'd smiled with frank appreciation. That Sunday she was wearing the new fur-felt hat that Annie had given her at Christmas. She'd been doubtful about the blue satin bow but she was glad now she'd given in to Annie's scolding and worn it. She could feel that the cold winter wind had whipped a tint into her normally pale face. She hoped it hadn't done the same to her nose.

In the other room, Annie stirred, muttering unintelligibly to herself, but she didn't wake. Millie wet the edge of the towel and rubbed hard at her cheeks and neck. She had to try to get into work today. She'd been forced to take two days off already this month because she felt so ill. One more and she'd lose the job. But the smell of the fermenting malt made her ill and faint. At first she hadn't eaten anything, hoping that would help. Then one morning, the woman who sat beside her at the long table leaned over and without preamble, but kindly, said, "You should eat something, dear, a crust of dry bread is the best. It always helped me." Milly had blushed, terrified at being found out.

She went over to the cupboard and took down the tin where she'd stashed the heels of bread. She forced herself to nibble on one of them. What was going to become of her? John had been so cold, so angry, when she and Annie had gone to the house. Because Mrs. Pedlow had told him to, he'd brought them into the kitchen and given them each a glass of lemonade. But ungraciously, wanting them gone. They hadn't stayed long. Just time enough for Annie to give him a piece of her mind.

"We'll see you on Sunday," Annie said. "And I expect you to have the banns called right away." Her voice was harsh and contemptuous, which had turned John even more sullen. Seeing that, Millie cringed. She herself wanted only to appease him.

She sat down at the table. Annie's supper plate wasn't washed, and the sight of the caked egg made saliva fill her mouth. She waited, sweating, until the nausea passed. The brown paper bag was still sitting where Annie had left it. What if she took the herbs? Tentatively, she ran her hands over her own breasts. Already they were swollen considerably, and the nipples were tender and sore. She remembered vividly Mrs. Reilly's pregnancies, the discomfort, the constant complaining. Both Millie and Annie had looked after the youngest ones as they came along, but the truth was Millie had often left them to cry untended in the soiled cradle. Annie had been better, almost always tender and loving.

Millie felt a rush of tears. She knew that without this one under her apron there was no reason for John to marry her and that thought was unbearable. She shifted restlessly in the chair. He'd seemed so much in love at first, showering her with dizzying attention. For a few weeks, he had been content to escort her home after church but then he began to hint this was not enough. One Sunday, she invited him in for tea, knowing Annie was not at home. They were sitting on the rickety couch that was jammed against the wall in the kitchen and he had slid to the floor, buried his face in her lap and with muffled voice had professed his love. He was beside himself with desire, he said. Did she love him in the same way? He thought she did, hoped beyond hope that she did. She couldn't speak, only touch his head as tentatively as if it were a burning coal. He kissed her then, so ardently she felt faint. And filled with joy she had never before known.

The next week, however, he avoided her eye and even though he walked her home, he was remote and unsmiling. She begged him to tell her what was wrong, to forgive her if she had offended him. Reluctantly, he told her. He was going mad with desire. He could neither eat nor sleep. If she loved him, she would show her love and give herself to him as a wife, in God's eyes if not the world's. Otherwise, he said with a sigh, he could not bear the pain a moment longer and he would be forced to break off their friendship. Sick with fear, she had agreed and, that very day, invited him into the shabby bedroom. Once there, she succumbed and was overcome with shame as her own ardour and yearning swept away through her body. He had liked that, he said, liked her passion. However, after they'd had connections four or five times, he confessed he was promised to someone else. He didn't love the other woman, a family promise, but he had to honour it. He had wept, caressing her until she was on fire and again and again she capitulated.

"Changed your mind?"

Annie had got out of bed and was standing in the doorway. Her face was puffy, her hair dishevelled, and even from here Millie could smell the reek of wine on her breath. But for once Annie's expression was soft and loving. Millie reached up her arms as if she were a child.

"Oh, Annie, I'm so afraid."

Her sister came over to her and pulled her close.

"Hush now. Don't cry anymore, little Sissie. I'll take care of things."

"How can you?" Millie sobbed.

"Shh. Shh. It will be all right, I promise. I haven't failed you yet, have I?"

Millie pressed against the soft, familiar breasts. She didn't want to acknowledge the strain and worry in Annie's face. She just wanted to feel safe again.

Freddie was trying not to touch George's body. The older boy had threatened him with dreadful retribution if he did. Or if he pissed in the bed. Freddie couldn't help when it happened in the night, and he was afraid to go to sleep. For the past three days, George had been in a dreadful bad skin. He had bought a jug of hard beer every day and by night-time he was full. Like Mrs. Mother his mood worsened the more he drank, and Freddie was an easy target for his wrath.

Curled up as tightly as he could be, Freddie was listening. The night was full of sounds; the tapping of the trees against the window, mice scrabbling in the wainscot, footsteps in the street. They all frightened him. He would like to have wakened George but he dared not. He wished Lily would come back. He was hungry. George had bought cream cakes and fat, sticky buns but after a while even they were not satisfying.

Not for the first time, Freddie wondered what was going to become of him.

It was after midnight when he finally dropped into sleep. He didn't hear the creaking of the back door nor the cautious steps as somebody moved across the kitchen.

CHAPTER FIFTEEN

CONSTABLE CRABTREE TAPPED ON THE WALL OUTSIDE Murdoch's cubicle, then popped his head through the reed curtain.

"Inspector would like to see you in his office, sir."

"This minute?" Murdoch was writing out his notes on what had happened so far with the Shaw case, and he was irritated at being interrupted.

"Yes, sir."

"What's he want?"

"He didn't say, sir." The constable answered the unspoken question. "He's a bit liverish this morning."

With a sigh, Murdoch got up and went upstairs to the

inspector's office.

Brackenreid was standing at his window looking into the street below. He didn't turn around.

"I swear that was Colonel Grasett's carriage going by. He told me he'd just bought a pair of fine greys."

"Really, sir? How splendid."

Brackenreid swung around, trying to see if he could pin down the offence he sensed in Murdoch's tone but not quite able to. Seeing his bewilderment, Murdoch felt a twinge of shame that he was baiting the man. Even though Brackenreid's snobbery galled him, it was like teasing a simpleton.

"You wanted to see me?" He forced himself to speak in a neutral voice.

The inspector sat down behind his desk. He'd removed his serge jacket and was wearing a short-sleeved fishnet undershirt. The thick hair on his chest poked through the holes. Murdoch thought he resembled a worn-down scrub brush. Omnipresent flies buzzed around the window and crawled across the big wooden desk. Murdoch was tempted to grab the swatter and send off a couple but he resisted. Why should he do Brackenreid's work? Last summer the inspector had assigned two of the youngest constables in the station to killing off all the flies. He'd fined them one cent for every fly he found alive.

Brackenreid squinted his eyes in a strange, leering way and, leaning forward in his seat, he said, "We have a spy and a saboteur in our midst and we must root him out at once."

Murdoch was taken aback.

"Sir?"

"Have you been paying attention to Crabtree's condition lately?"

"I beg your pardon, sir –"

"He doesn't look good. He's pasty, sluggish. When I asked him if anything was the matter, he said he's been having a touch of gastritis. Like hell he is."

He was trying so hard not to be overheard his voice was garbled and Murdoch could barely understand a word he said.

"Somebody is trying to poison him. Queer our chances in the pull. I'm convinced of it."

Murdoch stared at him. "Maybe he just has an upset stomach. Ate something that didn't agree with him."

"No. We went over everything that's gone into his mouth. Good wholesome food that his wife prepares. What he's always had."

"Why do you suspect poison?"

"Because a big, healthy man like him shouldn't be having bellyaches every day. Not like that. Somebody has made a wager against him and they want to make sure they win."

Brackenreid pulled at his moustache, putting the end in his mouth and sucking on it. "What's your opinion of Seymour? He's a sour puss. I've never trusted the man."

"I can't imagine it, sir. Sergeant Seymour is a thoroughly decent man."

"Even the best can be tempted, Murdoch. Even the best."

"If I may say, Inspector, the evidence is not conclusive that

Crabtree is being administered poison. Perhaps we should determine that before we look for a culprit."

Surprisingly, Brackenreid didn't lose his temper. "That's what I'm talking about, Murdoch. I want you to keep a close eye on him. I've instructed him not to eat or drink anything that his wife or you and me don't see first."

"All right."

"And I want you to taste everything before it goes into his mouth while he's here on duty."

"Sir?"

"Like Roman times. The emperors always had some slave sample their food first in case of poison."

"A slave!"

"Nothing wrong with that. They got to eat better than they would have normally."

"Unless they died first."

Brackenreid chuckled. "You'll be all right, Murdoch. You're clearly skeptical of the idea anyway. This'll put it to the test."

"I suppose it will."

"There's not a lot of time 'til the tournament. He's got to be in top shape."

Murdoch knew it was useless to try to reason with him. Once he had a bee in his bonnet, it would stay and buzz around there until it died of exhaustion.

"Is there anything else, sir?"

"No. You're proceeding with the River Street case, I presume?"

"Yes, sir."

Murdoch had not yet told Brackenreid about his interview with Mrs. Walter Pedlow. The inspector was jittery where Toronto's best society were concerned. If anything significant happened, Murdoch would tell him later.

"Have you nabbed the culprit yet?"

"Not yet, sir. The inquest was postponed until Friday because Mr. Johnson has the mumps."

"Does he? Poor fellow. That can do your member in forever. You can't get it up."

Murdoch thought he was wrong about that. He'd heard mumps could make you sterile but not impotent. However, he let it go. Brackenreid didn't like to stand corrected about anything.

"Find the daughter," the inspector continued. "She's the guilty party. Those cripples are like savages. No morals at all."

"She's not a cripple, sir. Just deaf."

"Same thing. Anyway, Murdoch, don't dawdle. Get to it. And by the by, don't mention a word to Crabtree. Don't want to make him jumpy. Just watch him the way a tigress watches her cub."

"Yes, sir. Like a tigress." He stood up. "Do you mind?"

He picked up the fly swatter and before the inspector could reply, smacked two or three flies in quick succession. He laid the swatter down on the desk.

"Thank you, sir. The bloody things are enough to drive a man to drink."

He left.

Mary Golding hadn't seen George or Fred since yesterday morning, but she'd fried some chicken patties for herself and John to have at tea and she decided to take some over to the two boys. Poor mites, as she constantly referred to them. She put the food into a dish with some boiled potatoes, pinned on her shawl, and walked across the road to Dolly's house. All the curtains were drawn, of course. She was glad she'd persuaded John to tack a black paper bow to the front door. Out of respect for Death, if not for Dolly Shaw.

She went up the steps, knocked on the door, and entered.

"Helloo! George! Freddie! It's Mrs. Golding."

There was no response at all. She called again, sniffing. There was a foul odour in the house. A smell she recognized from the time three years ago when she'd laid out her own mother. She assumed the rank stench lingered from Dolly. She really must help the boys clean up the place.

"Boys? Are you here? It's Mrs. Golding. I've brought you something for your tea."

The kitchen door was open. She was apprehensive now without quite knowing why. Cautiously, she entered the kitchen.

She was wrong about the origin of Death's stink. It wasn't from Dolly Shaw's corpse. The new source was the body which lay in a pool of blood in the middle of the kitchen floor.

Murdoch combed some brilliantine into his hair, smoothing out the waves at the sides. He also dabbed some on his moustache so that the hair shone sleek and dark. His cheeks and jaw were as smooth as soap and a sharp razor could make them. He tilted the mirror on the dresser and took another anxious scrutiny, holding up two of his silk four-in-hands. For the past ten minutes, he'd been vacillating between the brown check, which was conservative, and the olive with the Persian design, which was more flamboyant. He'd scattered all his ties on the bed and he dropped the two current favourites and picked up a black one with a yellow-and-red floral pattern. This was better, suggesting a man of basically sober character but not averse to adventure. Hurriedly, before he was again afflicted with indecision, he knotted the necktie around his high celluloid collar. He was going to be devilishly hot but it was worth it. Tonight he was off to attend Professor Otranto's salon. Permitted for the first time to join in with the other students at a real dance. He would be holding a real woman in his arms instead of his portly teacher.

With a final glance in the mirror, he slipped on his jacket. In anticipation of this event he'd splurged on a new cotton jacket with black and white stripes. He'd also bought a boater with a black band. He paused, not sure if the flowers in the tie went with the stripes. Too late now. It was already a quarter to eight and he'd better hurry. He planned to walk there as he didn't want to risk getting any bicycle grease on his white duck trousers. Also at the back of his mind, barely acknowledged, was the thought that he might escort one of the women students to her home afterwards. Easier to do that without a wheel.

He stuffed his patent leather dancing shoes into a brown

paper bag and smoothed his hair one last time. That was a mistake because he now had grease on his fingers. He wiped them off on his handkerchief.

Outside in the hall, he paused at Enid's open door. She was clacking away at the typewriting machine and the little boy was lying on the bed. At first he seemed asleep but he lifted his head and coughed hard. He had been feverish for the past two days and now the cough. Everybody was worried, especially Mrs. Kitchen, frightened lest the consumption be passed on.

Murdoch tapped gently on the door and Enid turned around, smiling with pleasure when she saw him.

"Mr. Murdoch. What a swell you look then."

He felt a rush of warmth himself. And a twinge of guilt.

"Thank you. I'm off to my dancing class. It's a special evening. All the pupils get to dance together."

"I see."

Was it his imagination or did she look a bit dashed?

"The professor has said we can bring a guest when we're more practised. Perhaps you would join me?"

"Thank you, Mr. Murdoch, but I don't dance."

He felt foolish. Of course she didn't dance. She was a staunch Baptist.

Then the boy coughed again, distracting them.

"How is he?" Murdoch asked.

"A little better. He hasn't wanted to eat anything at all, but Mrs. Kitchen made some toast water and he liked that."

"Good… well I'd better be off, I'm late as it is."

She turned back to her work. "Good evening then."

"Good evening. *Nos da.*"

That netted him such a lovely smile he hurried off, all aglow, down the stairs. Neither of the Kitchens was abroad and he was glad, too self-conscious about his nobby appearance to want comment.

Professor Otranto finished sorting out the music and clapped his hands. He was short and round, with soft cheeks that folded over his collar. His wife on the other hand was a good eight inches taller with a strong beaky nose and chin. Murdoch often speculated that the dance teacher took the woman's part in more than just the waltz.

"Now then, ladies and gentlemen, we are about to begin. Our first dance will be a two-step. Not too difficult for all of you, I'm sure. Mr. Cockbourne, would you be so good as to escort Miss Dickenson to the floor. She is the charming young lady at the far end of the row."

With alacrity Cockbourne went to claim his partner, who blushed as pink as the muslin carnations she'd fastened to her dress.

"Mr. Murdoch, your partner is Miss Kirkpatrick. She is seated next to Miss Dickenson."

Murdoch walked across the slick dance floor toward the young woman, who was beaming at him happily, her head slightly cocked to one side. She was wearing a black taffeta skirt with a high-necked silk blouse of magenta and green stripes, and he was put to mind of a little parrot he'd seen once on a sailor's shoulder. He offered her his arm.

"Miss Kirkpatrick, may I have the honour?"

She jumped up and he led her to the floor, where the others were getting in place.

"Isn't this jolly?" she said, and Murdoch smiled in agreement.

She smelled overpoweringly of lavender and seemed to be caught in a fit of the giggles but he was charmed by her unaffected delight.

"Ladies and gentleman, are you ready?" Otranto called out to them. The students quieted down at once.

Madame Otranto, who was to play the piano for them, struck a couple of chords, glanced around, then plunged into a vigorous two-step. The professor started the call.

"Dud-duh, duh, duh, dud-duh, duh, duh; dud-duh, dud-duh, duh, duh. Kick. And *slide, slide*. Mr. Walker, lightly please! And back, *slide, slide.*"

Miss Kirkpatrick's round cheeks were soon red with the exertion.

"Oh it's so jolly." She laughed. "My name's Clarice, what's yours?"

"Will," he managed to gasp out.

"Waltz coming up," shouted the professor. "And… one, two, three; one, two, three."

Murdoch remembered to hold his partner in correct dance position, his right hand in the centre of her back. She was very pliable. Otranto continued to count out the beat, and the dancers whirled. He hadn't made any mistakes so far; his partner's slippers were pristine.

"Advance," shouted Otranto, and while the women stayed in place, gracefully swaying with slightly lifted skirts, the men moved on around the circle. Murdoch executed that safely enough and skipped on to his next partner. She was short with abundant hair and for a moment made him think of Enid. She was too intent on dancing to smile, but he slipped his arm around her waist and went into the step.

"Tappedy, tappedy, tap, tap…"

He again managed the waltz perfectly and it was only as he progressed around the circle to meet his next partner that he became aware a man had entered the room and was standing by the door. A lanky man in a policeman's uniform. Startled, Murdoch did the unforgivable and trod on the heels of the person in front of him, who bellowed and started to hop on one foot. The couple who were following behind collided as well.

But even in the general confusion and rush of apologies, Murdoch saw the constable had beckoned to him.

CHAPTER SIXTEEN

MURDOCH REGRETTED HE'D LEFT HIS WHEEL AT HOME as he and Constable Wiggin jog-trotted up from King Street. In his hurry he'd forgotten to change out of his dancing slippers and by the time they reached the Shaw house, his feet felt bruised from contact with the macadam pavement. It was almost dark by now and the street lamps struggled feebly to overcome the dusk that had crept across the city. Once again a crowd of curious onlookers was gathered on the sidewalk outside the house.

"What's going on, Officer?" called out one of the men, seeing them approach. Murdoch recognized him. He'd been in exactly the same spot before.

"It's not the poor bairns, is it?" a woman asked.

"Don't know anything yet," said Murdoch. "Now let me through."

They did at once, then closed ranks behind him like the sea.

There were no lights showing inside, but the constable on guard at the doorstep had lit his dark lantern and he held it aloft, waving it like a beacon. Murdoch went up the steps.

"Wiggin, stay out here, please. Burney, show me where." The constable stepped back into the hall.

"In the kitchen, sir." The door was ajar.

"Let's have some more light," said Murdoch and waited while Burney fumbled for a match and lit the candle in the wall sconce. His hands were trembling. Murdoch drew a deep breath. He wasn't exactly calm himself.

"Give me your lantern, Dick."

He did and Murdoch entered the kitchen, holding the light up high.

The beam illuminated the body of George Tucker.

He was lying on his stomach next to the stove. His face was turned towards the door and a knife protruded from the junction of his neck and shoulder. His eyes were open and blood had gushed from his mouth so that there was a dark pool, thick with flies, all around his head. He was dressed only in a nightshirt, which had been soaked with blood.

Murdoch flashed the light around the room. It appeared undisturbed. He shouted to the constable.

"Burney, find me some more frigging candles, it's dark as the

Devil's asshole in here."

The constable came in, avoiding looking at the dead boy.

"There's one on the table," said Murdoch. He waited until Burney had lit the stub, then he went over to the body, knelt down, and touched the boy's cheek lightly with the back of his hand. The skin was cold and clammy. Burney edged closer.

"He's just a lad, isn't he, sir? Who would do such a thing?"

Murdoch stood up. "Up to us to find out, isn't it?"

He was being snappy but he couldn't help it. Protruding from the skimpy nightshirt, George's legs were scrawny, virtually hairless. He looked like a little child.

"There's another candlestick on that sideboard. Bring it over here and hold both of them close."

Murdoch placed the lantern on the table and together with the two candles, he had sufficient light for a cursory examination of the body. The skin was already blackening and the blood had congealed on the nightshirt.

Tenderly, as if it mattered, Murdoch moved the boy's head. It turned freely enough. He tested the arms and legs which had now lost the stiffness of death.

"Shine the lantern here a minute."

Burney, still shaky, brought the light closer to George's back. Murdoch could see a narrow puncture just between the shoulder blades. From the amount of blood that had flowed from the wound, he assumed the knife had pierced a lung. There didn't seem to be another wound except the final deadly blow to the neck. He examined both hands but there were no signs of cuts on the palms or fingers. No evidence of a struggle.

"See if there's a match to this knife in any of the drawers," he told Burney. He stood up. The kitchen was tidy enough except for a half-eaten loaf of bread and a rind of cheese on the table.

Burney was investigating the sideboard, and he held up a knife with a yellowish bone handle. It was identical to the murder weapon.

"There's two more in here, sir."

"Keep it out. We'll show it to the coroner. God, I need some air. Let's go into the hall. Leave the candles."

Burney followed him.

"You got some blood on your trousers, sir."

Murdoch looked down at his knee, which was stained.

"Damn it."

"Sorry we had to spoil your dance, Mr. Murdoch. The sergeant thought as it was your case, you should be gotten."

Murdoch moistened his handkerchief and wiped off the mark as best he could.

"I don't suppose you've checked the rest of the house, have you?" he asked the constable.

"No, sir."

"Come on then, there's two other people who live here normally. A boy and a woman. Let's see if they're with the quick or the dead."

He went to the centre of the hall and called.

"Hulloo? Anybody here? Freddie, it's Detective Murdoch… are you here? Don't be afraid."

The house was silent as only a place of death can be silent.

Murdoch approached the closed parlour door. Fear of what he might find made his stomach shrink but he had no choice. He thrust it open. Empty. It didn't look changed from when he'd last seen it.

"Let's go upstairs. Take that candle."

He led the way up to the narrow landing.

"Hello! Freddie, are you up here?" He paused, his voice sinking into the silence like ink on blotting paper. He nodded at Burney.

"I'll do it."

The door to the boy's room was partially open. He pushed it all the way, waited, then stepped inside. It was empty. He crouched down and shone the light underneath the bed. Nothing except for two pairs of worn boots and a full slop pail.

On the chair was a small pile of clothes, a pair of brown plaid trousers, and a holland shirt, shabby and torn. There was another bundle on the floor. Black serge trousers and a blue, well-patched shirt.

"Looks like Freddie ran off without his clothes," he said to Burney who was standing at the threshold.

"D'you think he's the one done it, sir? They might have had a row, lad snatches up the carving knife. Then nub nux. Didn't mean to do it, but too late now, isn't it?"

Murdoch shrugged. He didn't think so. For one thing, Freddie was smaller than George and he'd seemed a timid lad. On the other hand, sometimes the worm will turn. Perhaps the boy had been provoked beyond endurance. He hoped that wasn't what had happened.

"Looks bad on him if he has done a bunk. He'd be here if he's innocent," added the constable.

"Or he could be dead too."

"Maybe it was a kelp as did the lad in, then. Maybe the old lady had a stash hidden somewhere. Same person as did for her, came back to bird the loot. The boy surprised him. Slam. He's done for."

"If he came upon a burglar why was he stabbed in the back?"

"Maybe he was trying to get away?"

"He's not facing the door. He must have been going towards the cupboard."

"Could have been terrified into next year. Ran blindly."

"I don't think he'd be that confused in his own house." Murdoch stepped back. "All right. There's nothing else to get here. We'll take a better gander in the daylight. Let's see the other room."

They went across the landing. Once again Murdoch pushed open the door and shone in the lantern before entering. The room was just as he'd left it. Tidy. Empty.

He turned back to the constable. "Get off to the station and tell Sergeant Seymour to call up the coroner. Johnson has the mumps so it'll have to be Mr. Vaux. We'll need the police ambulance. I'll check out the backyard and the privy."

"Do you think we're looking for soul cases or live folks?"

"I don't know, Dick. I wish I did."

Murdoch put his glass on the table. The Goldings' neighbour Mrs. Daly had come to be with Mrs. Golding and had brought over a jug of homemade raspberry vinegar, which she claimed was the best thing for fright. Murdoch was handed a glass as soon as he came in. It was certainly reviving, and Mrs. Golding was looking better by the minute. He could detect generous amounts of brandy but if Mrs. Golding was aware this was in the recipe, she didn't protest.

"Some more, Mr. Murdoch?" Mrs. Daly asked, picking up the jug.

"No, thank you, ma'am, that was plenty for me. And delicious if I may say so."

The neighbour looked pleased. She turned to Mrs. Golding who was getting quite flushed. "Mary?"

"I don't think so, thank you, Philomena."

"Nonsense. You've had the most dreadful fright. One more will put you right." She poured another large glassful and Mary took a gulp.

When Murdoch first arrived, she had indeed been in a state of nervous prostration. Mrs. Daly was waving a bottle of sal volatile under her nose, causing Mary to cough and choke alarmingly. When she was sufficiently recovered, however, she had managed to give her story coherently enough. She hadn't seen either of the boys since the previous evening when she'd noticed both of them walking along Wilton Street towards the house. She hadn't heard any sound at all from them after that.

She knew definitely it was six o'clock when she'd gone over, because she wanted to make sure she was back in plenty of time to serve Mr. Golding's tea at half past six.

"They seemed such little orphans," she repeated. She'd already said that but it was as if the observation was fresh each time.

"Ragamuffins, if you ask me," said Mrs. Daly. "They weren't Dolly's own children, that was clear. Heathens more than likely, with no conscience. That's what comes of being brought up with no Christian guidance."

Mary Golding wiped away more tears that kept spilling from her eyes. Her words were slightly slurred. "The older boy, the one who is dead, he could be quite savage to the other child. Just yesterday, I saw him hit him so hard the poor little mite almost fell over."

"Poor little mite indeed! That same mite is likely to grow up a candidate for the old nevergreen."

Murdoch looked at the three people in front of him. John Golding was across the road with the coroner. He'd been sworn as a juror and was presently viewing the body. Clarence Daly was sitting in the corner. So far he'd said nothing and his wife acted as if he weren't there at all.

"You are all certain that you heard nothing in the Shaw house, around eleven or twelve last night?" Murdoch asked them.

He'd already had their answers but sometimes it was worth another prod. Mrs. Daly looked as if she would have manufactured something if she could but she shook her head reluctantly.

"No, Mr. Daly and me were in our Christian beds at ten o'clock on the dot and slept as sound as planks, didn't we, Clarence?"

Her husband hesitated. "Well, I could have heard somebody crying out."

"What do you mean crying out? You were fast asleep like me. How could you?"

Mr. Daly shuffled his feet, torn between the fear of displeasing his wife and being important in the eyes of the police.

"I had to get up, see..." More shuffle. "Excuse me, Mary. I had to use the commode. Our bedroom window was open and I thought I heard a cry. Didn't know if it was a cat or what. There's one that keeps coming around and smelling up our front porch."

He had everybody's attention now and it gave him confidence.

"Why didn't you say this before?" said Murdoch.

"I've been sitting here athinking when it was I got up, and it probably was close to midnight. But like I says, I thought it was a tom."

"Don't dither, Clarence Daly, was it a cat or a human soul?" His wife spoke with asperity.

"I'd say now as I've considered the matter, it was a human cry."

"Male or female?" Murdoch asked.

"Not sure, sir. But perhaps more likely the weaker vessel."

"Can you describe the sound more exactly?" asked Murdoch.

Daly put back his head and to everybody's astonishment let out a strange howling.

"Clarence!" exclaimed his wife, as if he'd done something as shameful as pull down his trousers in public.

"That's the kind of cries the dummy would make," said Mrs. Golding.

Philomena nodded. "You're right about that, Mary. It is like."

Pleased with himself, Clarence bayed again. It was a similar sound to the cry that had come from Lily when Murdoch and Crabtree appeared at the house last Thursday.

"Did you see Mrs. Shaw's daughter?"

"No. Didn't look out or anything. Could have been her. Could have been that cat that's been prowling around, stinking up the porch."

"Must have been Lily," said his wife. "Another heathen."

"Have you seen anything at all of Miss Shaw?" Murdoch asked Mrs. Golding.

"Not since her mother passed on."

"Seems to me Lily did in her own flesh and blood and then murdered the foster child. I always knew she was a madwoman," said Mrs. Daly.

"I didn't," interjected Clarence, emboldened. "Just seemed like a poor afflicted soul to me."

Murdoch jumped in before a quarrel could start. "She's disappeared. If it was her that you heard, we'd like to talk to her. Do you have any idea where she might be hiding? And the other boy? Any relatives or particular friends that you know of who might take him in?"

"Not a one," answered Mrs. Daly. "They had hardly any company. She wasn't the sort of woman we wanted to associate with. When she first came here to live we did, of course, make overtures, didn't we, Mary?"

Mrs. Golding nodded and Mrs. Daly went on.

"We called on her." She tightened her mouth at the memory. "First off, she seemed to be thoroughly intoxicated even though it was only two o'clock in the afternoon; secondly –"

"She took us into her parlour." Mary Golding joined in eagerly now. "She didn't offer us any refreshment or make any enquiries but right away she began to talk about the furniture and how grand it was."

"That was the drink –"

"She said she used to be grand herself, a professional woman, she said, but she had fallen on hard times through no fault of her own."

"What had happened?" asked Murdoch.

"She didn't say." Mrs. Daly took back the narrative, firmly. "Just made all sorts of hints that her own daughter had brought about her ruin. Mary and me didn't know what to think –"

"Poor unfortunate girl."

"Then she began to brag on and on about the people she knew. Society people she said. Well, I am a charitable person, Mr. Murdoch, but frankly I didn't believe a word of it."

"Neither did I." Mrs. Golding tried to insert herself back in the conversation, with no success.

"She must have sensed our reservations," added Philomena. "The next thing we knew she had gone to a big desk that was under the window. She had the key on a cord around her neck." Mrs. Daly pursed her lips again. "She brought out an autograph album. The way she handled it, you'd think she had signatures from the royal family –"

"She said it was her record book –" piped Mary, very flushed now.

"That's right. I asked her, 'A record of what?' 'Of the signs of the world,' she said and gave the most unpleasant sort of laugh –"

"Gave me the shivers. I mentioned it to John when I came home –"

Philomena interrupted. "At that moment, the poor dummy came in with some tea and Mrs. Shaw screamed at her. I've never seen such appalling behaviour."

Mrs. Golding nodded vigorously. "She said Lily had brought in the wrong cups."

"No, it was on the wrong tray. Regardless, it was quite unreasonable. Absolutely nothing would please her. The dummy, of course, couldn't say anything. It was like seeing somebody beat a dog in public. Mary and I left as soon as we could."

Mrs. Golding agreed. Mrs. Daly rumbled on.

"After that we wouldn't subject any other Christian women to that treatment. We warned all the other ladies in the neighbourhood. Virtually no one else called on her. She made herself half decent for a while but only when she wanted to borrow something."

"Money?" Murdoch asked.

"Yes, and household goods. I lent her one of my frying pans and I've yet to see it. Any money you might as well consider a charity gift."

"What did the record book look like?"

"It was yellow," said Mrs. Golding.

"No, dear. Forgive me but that is not correct. The book was green, Mr. Murdoch. Covered with silk moire I'd say."

"Leather," muttered Mary.

"The boys liked to play by the river," said Mr. Daly suddenly. "I've seen them coming back with fish. The darkie might have run off there to hide."

Mrs. Golding looked up out of her handkerchief where she had taken temporary respite. "Do you think something has happened to him, Mr. Murdoch? Something bad?"

"I don't know, ma'am. It's possible he witnessed the murder and ran off in fear of his life or –"

Daly said, "He could have killed George himself and done a bunk."

"I can't believe that. He is just a child…" Mary's voice trailed off.

"She's very soft-hearted, Mr. Murdoch. Weeps if a bird dies. But we can't deceive ourselves, Mary. The boy might be dead too, buried somewhere…"

"Mr. Murdoch, is that so?"

"I'm afraid it's not out of the question, Mrs. Golding."

"I tell you, Officer," interjected Mrs. Daly. "Me and Clarence are strong churchgoers, Methodist. I never saw Dolly Shaw step foot on even so much as the threshold of any church that I know of. None of them did. I hate to say it, but no doubt justice was done. The wicked shall get their due."

That didn't sound quite right to Murdoch but maybe it was a Methodist saying.

Freddie had run to the empty house next to them, squeezing between the planks that boarded up the door. He cowered in the corner of the kitchen for hours, expecting to be discovered at any moment. No one came, and after a long time he almost wished they would.

He was so hungry he was sucking on his knuckles as if he were a baby. His stomach hurt. There was a pile of old potato sacks against the wall and he slept on those even though they smelled of mice droppings and sour food. He dared not go outside in case someone saw him, so he had relieved himself in the farthest corner, covering it as best he could with some straw that was scattered about the floor. He moaned constantly, almost unaware that he was doing so. He had no plan, could think of nothing except how to survive the next moment and then the next.

CHAPTER SEVENTEEN

MURDOCH RETURNED TO THE SHAW HOUSE FIRST THING the next morning. George's body had been moved to the undertakers on Yonge Street, but where he had lain was demarcated by the stencil of congealed blood on the oilcloth. Murdoch went over to the place, standing in the clean area as much as possible. He was near the large pine cupboard. One of the doors was unfastened and he opened it. Inside were a few plates and bowls, some chipped mugs. He pretended to reach for something. One blow from behind, he staggered forward; another blow to the neck and he crumbled to the floor, falling sideward. His position fitted exactly with the angle of George's body and suggested his assailant had come from around the table. Was that who was eating the bread and cheese? It didn't make sense that George had surprised a stranger, some thief breaking in for a bit of supper. He would not have advanced into the room if he perceived he was in danger.

Murdoch sat down at the table, taking the chair that faced the door. The used plate was directly in front of him, the loaf of bread at his right hand. The murder weapon was a bread knife. What seemed likely was that George entered the kitchen, saw the person, but wasn't perturbed enough to turn and run. In fact, at some point he went toward the cupboard. Was there a quarrel? Some provocation so severe that the other person snatched the bread knife, ran at George from behind and delivered two powerful blows. The first wound punctured the lung and a fine spray of blood had covered the corner of the table. There were several sheets hanging on a rack between the windows. The ones closest to the cupboard looked as if they had been dyed pink. Murdoch rubbed one of them between his fingers. It was good quality linen. Somebody was going to be missing their laundry soon.

Given that the murder looked like an unpremeditated act, Murdoch expected that the killer panicked and ran out, most likely by the shortest route to the door. That would take them right across the path of the body and the blood. He crouched down and moved slowly forward. Nothing that he could see, just some scuff marks and bits of mud which were probably left by the jurors who had viewed the body.

He spent the next half hour examining the kitchen, but

could find nothing else that seemed relevant to the murder. He was glad to move on to the rest of the house. Re-enacting the attack had brought back disturbing memories. He knew the shock and pain of an unexpected blow. His father had landed many of them. Worse had been the sight of his young brother, Albert, knocked senseless for some misdemeanour he had no awareness of. Murdoch's own rage churned biliously in his stomach. It had not diminished after all these years. Murderous anger was an emotion he could understand.

He went into the parlour, opening the curtains this time and thrusting up all the window sashes. Mrs. Daly had spoken about an album. An important book by the sound of it. He hadn't seen it the first time he examined the room but he had more idea now of what he was looking for.

For the next hour he searched thoroughly, taking up the carpet, a once-luxurious Axminster, moving aside all the grand furniture. Nothing. He wondered if he'd misinterpreted the money in Dolly's pocket. Perhaps she herself intended to pay somebody. According to the neighbours she owed money. Maybe one of her creditors got fed up with waiting. Lost his temper and sent her off. That possibility didn't sit right though, and he felt frustrated. Once again there were too many paths to go down. He left and went upstairs.

Lily's room was untouched as far as he could see but he sieved through it again just in case. It yielded nothing.

The boys' room was also the same as he'd seen it last. He'd done no more than a perfunctory search before. The room was so bare and, at that point, he didn't suspect either of the two boys. Perhaps he was wrong. He remembered the whispers while he was in Lily's room. Were they hiding evidence? If so, what?

When he was about George's age he'd started to steal tobacco plugs from his father. His father hadn't seemed to notice and young Murdoch chawed away, savouring not the bitter taste but the defiance, the secret victory. He kept the stash under his mattress and was never found out.

Murdoch went over to the bed and with a heave turned over the mattress. It was filthy but intact, and nothing lay underneath it on the iron bedsprings. However, the one pillow fell to the floor and he could see wool stuffing dribbling out of one end. He picked it up and patted it. There was something firm in the middle. Too small to be the album, but something hidden. He fished inside and his fingers came in contact with what felt like a roll of paper. He pulled it out in a flurry of wool bits which stuck to his fingers like Golding's tubercles. He shook them off and unwrapped the bundle, which was in a piece of the *Globe*. Inside was a wad of bills, mostly one dollar in denomination. He counted them. Forty-three dollars. He couldn't believe the money was George's or Freddie's. They would be lucky to have twenty-five cents to their name. He probed the pillow's innards again and this time plucked out a leather cord at the end of which dangled a small brass key. Looked like the missing desk key.

He riffled the notes. Forty-three dollars wasn't a lot of money but perhaps enough to kill for if you were as destitute as these boys were. He folded the wad and put it in one of his envelopes.

He would have discarded the newspaper, but suddenly a photograph caught his eye. A group of people on a lawn. In the centre was his honour, Walter Pedlow, seated with a rug over his legs. A younger man was to his right. Murdoch peered closer. The picture was fuzzy but he recognized this fellow. He was the one who had partnered Annie Brogan at the Derby. The too-long hair and thick moustache were unmistakable. He read the caption. "His honour, Walter Pedlow, at the reception of his nephew, Henry, recently returned from India. Mrs. Walter Pedlow is to the left of her husband and their ward, Miss Sarah Carswell, is directly in front of her."

Maud had her head turned away from the camera. Somebody had circled the child's face.

Murdoch felt a flush of excitement. *Don't tell me there's no connection between Dolly Shaw and the Pedlows. Never heard of the woman, my eye! And why is Henry Pedlow hanging around Annie Brogan if they're all such total strangers?* The date of the paper was at the top, Wednesday, July 17, and there was a brownish stain across the side that looked like blood. He placed it in the envelope with the money.

There was nothing else in the room, just the fetid stink of misery.

It was approaching noon when he got back to the station. As he entered, the duty sergeant, Seymour of the sour puss, called him over.

"Package for you, Will, just arrived."

He handed him a large brown envelope. It had the coroner's seal on the back and Murdoch took it with him to his cubicle at the rear. He felt as if the smell of death clung to his clothes and he removed his jacket, putting it on the peg by the door. Her Majesty watched him benignly.

Vaux, the coroner, had sent on a copy of the doctor's post mortem examination.

This is to certify that I, Robert Joseph Grieg, a legally qualified physician of the city of Toronto, did this day make a post mortem examination upon the body of a person identified as George Tucker, with the following result.

The body is that of a youth of about thirteen years of age, undernourished. Genitalia is mature. Rigor mortis was resolving with some remaining rigidity in the feet. Abdominal organs, kidneys, normal in size. There were signs of worm infestation in the lower bowel. Both legs were curved concavely. In my opinion evidence of childhood rickets. The entire chest cavity and pleura were filled with blood, the result of two stab wounds to the back, one close to the left scapula, and approximately seven and one half inches below the occiput, the other slightly higher, that is six inches from the occiput but the same distance from the scapula. Both wounds punctured the left lung. The third wound was at the junction of the left clavicle and the thoracic vertebrae. This wound severed the aorta. The knife had penetrated to a depth of four inches. Most of the body's blood had drained from these wounds. The murder weapon is an ordinary kitchen knife with a sawtooth edge and a bone handle. In my opinion all blows were administered with great force from above by a person who is right-handed. Respectfully submitted, Robert Grieg M. D.

The language was cool and clinical, as it should be, but Murdoch felt troubled by what it meant in human terms. Dr. Grieg had written, "genitalia mature", but George Tucker was far from adulthood in size and strength. He'd had so little comfort in his short life and the brutality of his death was surely undeserved.

Murdoch returned the report to the envelope and stood up. He needed to be active. He left his cubicle and went to the off-duty room to see who was there. Crabtree was sitting at the table and he was about to take a big swallow from a bottle of stout.

"Wait!"

Startled, Crabtree halted, the bottle held in mid-air.

"Let me have a sip, I'm parched."

Surprised, Crabtree handed over the bottle. Murdoch paused. He thought Brackenreid was as full of wind as a barber's cat but… he sniffed at the bottle, the rich smell of stout wafting up to him. What now? If he himself dropped dead in violent spasms it wouldn't necessarily help Crabtree. The constable was watching him curiously.

"Something wrong, sir?"

"Did you open this yourself?"

"Yes, sir."

"What are you eating?"

"Some bread and ham that my wife put up." He looked uneasy. "You've been talking to the inspector, haven't you? He keeps dropping these peculiar hints that somebody is trying to poison me."

"It's not out of the question," Murdoch said reluctantly. "How's your stomach?"

"Not too good, sir. Bit of the cramps."

While he was speaking, he took out a small pillbox and shook four green-coloured tablets into his palm.

"What's that?"

"Strengthening pills the inspector gave me. He got them from the Sears catalogue. Special order."

"Can I have a look?"

Crabtree gave him the pillbox and Murdoch sniffed at it.

"Smells like almonds."

"That's the flavouring."

"Hey, hold on, Crabtree, it says here to take four a day. At intervals. Why are you taking them all at once?"

"I'm not exactly. The inspector recommended that I increase the dosage seeing as I'm big. I'm taking four pills six times a day."

"Maybe you should cut it back. They may be upsetting your stomach."

Crabtree looked dubious. "The inspector was insistent, Mr. Murdoch. You know how he is."

"I certainly do. Look, lend me the box for a couple of hours.

I'll do a bit of research."

"I don't think –"

"I'll take full responsibility."

"All right. But I wouldn't take too long if I were you, sir."

Murdoch put the pillbox in his pocket.

"I'm off to see the Brogan woman. See what she has to say for herself this time."

"Dreadful to think of that poor lad being done in like he was."

"I want to make sure the other young titch isn't going to be sent off either. If he's still alive that is. Crabtree, don't buy any apples from ugly old women."

"Sir?"

"Never mind, just joking you."

Murdoch left, realizing he hadn't tasted the stout and feeling like a yellow coward as a result.

Mr. Bright the druggist was standing in exactly the same place behind the counter as when Murdoch had seen him previously. He beamed a smile of recognition as the detective entered the shop.

"I've another request, Mr. Bright."

"Ask away. Anything to help safeguard the law."

Murdoch gave him the pillbox.

"Can you tell me what are the ingredients of these tablets?" He paused and glanced around the little shop. "A man's life could be saved. A good man, too. A strong Christian."

The druggist looked solemn, as befitted the responsibility.

"I'll run some tests. Can't get back to you 'til later this afternoon, though."

"That would be fine. I'll drop by."

"You don't need to. We've a telephone put in. Just last week. See?" He pointed proudly behind him where a shiny black walnut box was fastened to the wall. "I can call you up at the station as soon as I've done."

Murdoch thanked him. He felt obliged to show his appreciation more tangibly because he didn't think Mr. Bright had much custom.

"Do you have anything for sweetening the breath?"

"Wife complained, has she?"

Murdoch murmured unintelligibly.

"Is it teeth or tobacco? Causing the problem, I mean. If it's teeth, I've got whole line of homeopathic tinctures that'll take away pain and odour both. If it's tobacco, I've got some cachous that'd make Beelzebub himself acceptable."

"Should work for me then. I'll take a tin of those."

Warming to his task, Mr. Bright began to suggest other remedies for ills that Murdoch sincerely hoped he'd never have. He managed to withstand the Peruvian wine of coca for strengthening and the electricating liniment for sprains but succumbed to a few sticks of olive wax pomatum for his hair.

His package stuffed in his pocket, he edged out of the shop, Mr. Bright still suggesting medicines he might like.

As he stepped outside, he almost collided with a young woman who was walking at a brisk pace down Parliament Street.

He tipped his hat. "Sorry, ma'am."

Initially the woman was prepared to be cross at his clumsiness, but suddenly she smiled up at him.

"Mr. Murdoch. What a surprise."

For a moment, he didn't recognize the chubby, rose-cheeked face below him, then he realized it was his dancing partner from the previous evening. She was soberly dressed today in a charcoal-coloured silk cape and black skirt. Only in the crimson plumage and cherries that decorated her straw hat were there indications of the little exotic bird he'd danced with.

"Miss er…"

"Kirkpatrick. Clarice. I do hope the matter wasn't too dreadfully serious that made you run off like that."

"Unfortunately, it was."

She gazed up at him curiously but he didn't elaborate. He never talked about police work if he could avoid it. People had very odd reactions.

"Where are you off to in such a hurry?" he asked her.

"I'm going to work." She giggled a little. "I'm always late and today won't be any exception." She pointed down the street. "I work at Heineman's on King Street. I sing the latest songs for people to hear before they purchase the sheet."

"How marvellous."

"You should come and hear me sometime. You can pretend to be a customer. They'll never know."

"Thank you. I will."

Miss Kirkpatrick had pretty blue eyes which were twinkling

at him, but she wasn't a coquette, rather a simple, open-hearted young woman.

"Promise?"

He smiled. "I promise."

"And will you be at the next dance party?"

"Only a tidal wave would stop me."

The red cherries bounced a little as she lowered her head with a blush.

"I'll say good afternoon then, and be on my way. I don't want to get sacked."

Murdoch watched her briefly, admiring the jauntiness of her steps. The encounter warmed him. He sighed and retrieved his wheel from the curb. He didn't expect his next meeting would be as pleasant.

CHAPTER EIGHTEEN

AS MURDOCH CROSSED THE INTERSECTION OF PARLIAMENT and Queen, two boys dashed in front of him, kicking an inflated pig's bladder back and forth between them. They were ordinary-looking boys, reasonably well cared for, and he thought about the boy who no longer had a future of any kind. He'd pay for a Mass for his soul when he went to church on Sunday. Distracted, he didn't dodge the fresh horse droppings in the road and the bits of manure flew up into his face. He cursed.

He cycled past the Derby, which was quiet, not open for business yet. Close by, the foundry was belching salmon-coloured angry smoke. Thor with stomach ache. Or a case of poisoning.

On Front Street, he turned east and immediately hit the

strong cool wind from the lake. Pushing against it was like riding uphill. His legs were aching from this morning's hard training ride and he didn't feel like another challenge. He cursed again.

The steel-blue lake glittered in the sun, and a steamer chugged and puffed on its way, heading for Buffalo. A fat, dark plume of smoke, more tranquil than the foundry, was drifting from the tall stacks of the Gooderham and Worts Distillery, which was busy making the devil's brew, as Mr. Golding would have called it. In spite of the fact Murdoch disliked the self-righteous stance of so many Temperance folk, he also had some sympathy with their views. He'd seen what drunkenness did. His own father for one. As a young man, Murdoch had, in fact, taken the pledge. He'd lasted six months full of virtue, might have gone on to be an unbearable prig until he was offered a swig of cool ale at the end of a strenuous day of chopping. He was seduced and was conquered. Nothing he could remember had ever tasted as good as that smooth brew against his parched throat.

He was on Cherry Street now and he turned south, past a long trim warehouse. Opposite, close to the lakeshore, was the big distillery and the sweet smell of the whiskey was on the wind.

Mill Street was a narrow dirt road, dotted profusely with mounds of manure. It was the route to and from the distillery and many huge draft horses plodded by daily. The Brogan sisters lived at the end of a row of workmen's cottages. Theirs was distinguished by the height and abundance of the weeds that grew in front.

He must have pounded on the door for several minutes and was about to give up when Annie finally came to answer.

Shielding her eyes from the light, she squinted at him.

"What now?"

"Can I come in?"

She shrugged. "If you want to. The place isn't too tidy. I haven't got going yet."

He stepped inside. The front door opened directly into the one room of the house, where she and her sister obviously slept. Annie dumped a pile of undergarments off the single chair.

"Here, sit down. I'd offer you some char but we're all out. My sister isn't the best manager in the world. She's at work now." She nodded in the direction of the window. "At the distillery. She glues the labels on the bottles." She yawned. "Could you stand me a bit of shag? I'm all out of that too."

"You mean tobacco?"

"That's it."

Murdoch took out his tobacco pouch and shook some Badger into her open hand. She reached over to the washstand and picked up a clay pipe.

"You can have a smoke too," she said. "I don't mind."

"Not right now."

He waited while she lit up and took a deep draw. She was the first woman he'd ever seen smoking and it was odd. As if Mr. Kitchen would take up crocheting.

Through the fug she smiled at him. "Why should men have all the fun? I find it calming, don't you?"

"Yes, I do."

"All right, Mr. Murdoch. What's happened now?"

He got straight to the point.

"There's been another death. A murder."

"What are you talking about?"

"Last night we found the body of a young boy. His name was George Tucker and he was Mrs. Shaw's foster son."

"My God. What happened?" She was gazing at him in horror.

"Do you mean how was he killed?"

"Yes. Was it a fight?"

"Possibly. He was stabbed to death."

"My God," she said again. "But who would do that to a child?"

"He wasn't exactly a child. He must have been thirteen or fourteen."

She tamped down the tobacco in the pipe with the end of a spoon, not looking at him. "That's dreadful. I'm real sorry to hear it." More agitated tamping. "But why've you come here? What's it got to do with me?"

"That's for you to tell me."

"Mr. Murdoch. For Christ's sake. I've already told you I didn't know the woman, let alone this nipper."

"That's what you said, but you never know, things come back to us after a while. And seeing as how I'd come before, I thought it only right I should tell you what happened. See if in the shock, as it were, your memory got jogged."

"How could it if there was nothing there in the first place?"

"'Course we don't know yet why the boy was killed, but it's

highly likely the two deaths are connected."

"How d'you mean?"

"He probably knew something. Maybe even knew who killed his foster mother. Saw somebody!"

Annie's pipe was unheeded, about to go out. "Look. Let me scrounge around a bit. Maybe I can find some char. Cheer us both up, won't it."

She went into the tiny adjoining room and he heard her banging cupboards around.

"Good news," she called to him. "Millie was hiding some on me. There's enough for both of us."

"You have it. I've had mine already."

"Suit yourself."

More thumping. The sound of a poker in a grate. She came back into the living room.

"It'll just take a minute for the kettle to boil."

Plopping down on the bed, she reached for the pipe.

"Other than me, do you have any suspects?"

"Dolly's daughter is still missing. She's a likely one."

"If anybody had a reason to off Dolly Shaw, she did."

"Why's that?"

Annie froze, realizing what she'd said.

"You told me the old lady was cruel to her daughter."

"I don't remember saying anything of the kind."

"Yes, you did. How would I know otherwise?"

"Exactly my thought."

Suddenly the kettle whistled shrilly, and she jumped up

to tend to the tea. He heard the clink of cup and saucer, the vigorous stirring of the pot.

She came back carrying a tea tray, but she had regained her composure and she was once again in control of the situation. An entertainer who knew how to command attention. Murdoch didn't know how to get back his advantage.

"I remember now," she said, rather coyly. "It wasn't you who told me, it was the manager at the Derby. I had to explain what you were doing there. He knew somebody who lived up near Dolly. She'd told him about the daughter and how bad her mother treated her. Here."

She handed him a cup, which was quite elegant except for a long crack on one side and a saucer that didn't match. Murdoch had a sense of unreality. Here he was sitting next to a woman's unmade bed, that woman barely clothed, constantly revealing generous amounts of flesh, offering him tea in a fine china cup.

"Eager, are we?"

"What?"

"You said you didn't want tea and now look at you, snatching at it."

Her glance actually flickered over his crotch. Murdoch felt a rush of anger up his back.

"Miss Brogan, I'm a police detective investigating two violent deaths. Now maybe that's nothing extraordinary to you but it is to me. I don't want tea or anything else you're offering. I'd just like some straight answers."

She actually flushed. "You don't have to get funny. I'm

sorry about the boy, but I can't help you. I never seen him or the old woman."

"And you're sticking to that story?"

"Frigging right. It's my word against the sodding blind neighbour. You can't prove anything either way."

She stirred her tea with the handle end of a knife. "Besides, it don't mean that the woman who went into the house, if there was such a bint, it don't necessarily follow that she was the gallows finder, does it?"

"No, it doesn't. But it might be very helpful to talk to her."

Annie kept stirring. "We could all do with a bit of help in this world, couldn't we?"

"One more question, Annie. Why is Henry Pedlow paying court to you?"

She looked at him blankly. "Who's he when he's at home?"

"Mrs. Pedlow's nephew by marriage. He's the fellow who was waiting outside your dressing room the other day." She still looked puzzled. "He danced with you. Right after me. Dark hair, long. Sallow complexion."

"Jules! Gave his name as Jules LaVerne."

"He's Henry Pedlow. He's just got back from India."

For the first time, she appeared frightened. "What's he doing hanging around me?"

"That's what I'd like to know. What did he want?"

Annie stared at him for a moment, tried to look cynical, but her expression was weary.

"What'd you think? What you want, what they all want. But

don't worry. I wasn't interested in that dried-up piece of shoe leather."

"I wasn't. Worried, I mean."

Annie shrugged. "He said he wanted to send me red roses as an expression of his appreciation and admiration."

"That's it?"

"That's a lot for starters. Flowers now, next the best French bon-bons, then a nice pair of combs. Why are you men so predictable? You can have all the evil thoughts you like. Flog yourself with them if you want. I'm not for hire. I go with whoever I choose."

At that moment there was a loud knocking at the door.

"Annie! Annie! Rise and shine, my girl."

She jumped up. "Mother of God! That's a gentleman friend who's coming to take me to luncheon. Don't want him to see me like this."

She turned her back, undoing her dressing robe as she went towards the paper screen that was in the corner of the room. There she paused, and said over her shoulder, "Go tell him I'll be just a minute, there's a good-heart."

The robe slipped just below her plump, naked buttocks and she held it draped there for a second. An excellent exit.

The eager suitor knocked again, thunderously.

"Annie. Get up or I'll break the door down."

"Please Mr. Murdoch," said Annie from behind the screen. "Shut him up or we'll have the landlord in here. He lives in the next house."

Annoyed, Murdoch went to answer the door. The young man outside had his fist lifted ready to thump once more and he froze in mid gesture.

"Who are you?" he asked belligerently.

"A police officer and if you don't quiet down I'll have you up on a charge of drunk and disorderly."

"I'm not drunk," said the man. He was wearing a wide-brimmed hat and a bird's eye cravat. A country boy if ever there was one.

"Go to the end of the street and wait there. Silently. You sound like a bull in rut. She'll be there in a minute."

"Less than that," said Annie and she stepped from the screen. She had dressed very quickly indeed and she was still pinning up her hair as she came to the door.

"Thomas, you are a one. I'm ready." She glanced at Murdoch. "I wish you luck with the case."

Thomas beamed in triumph and offered her his arm. They walked off, leaving Murdoch to close the door behind them as if he were the butler.

CHAPTER NINETEEN

THIS TIME BURNS WAS MUCH FRIENDLIER, EAGER FOR a tidbit of gossip he could pass on to the rest of the servants.

"How is the enquiry coming along…?"

He couldn't quite get his mouth around *sir*, but his tone was conciliatory.

"Proceeding."

Disappointed with his response, Burns pursed his lips.

"I'll see if madam is at home."

He was about to go slithering off when Murdoch stopped him.

"I wonder if you'd do me a favour and just announce me."

The butler eyed him dubiously. "They won't like it."

"Tell them I insisted. You had no choice. I'll vouch for you."

Burns contemplated the pleasure of discomfiting his employer and the displeasure of the possible consequences. Pleasure won out.

"They're in the sun room taking afternoon tea. I recommend you don't linger. His honour doesn't like to be interrupted."

He led the way through the drawing room where Murdoch had previously met with Maud Pedlow. French doors opened onto the veranda, and here Burns gave a discreet tap and rather showily opened them.

"I beg your pardon, your honour, Mrs. Pedlow, Mr. Pedlow, but Detective Murdoch of number-four station wishes to speak to you."

Give him his due, Burns did announcements particularly well.

Murdoch heard a querulous voice say, "Not now, Burns, what are you thinking of..." but he entered right at the butler's shoulder.

Judge Pedlow, napkin tucked into his collar, was in the midst of stuffing a cake into his mouth. The cream had squeezed out around his lips like rabid foam. Maud Pedlow was seated beside him and across from her was Henry Pedlow. He looked at Murdoch in dismay and immediately lowered his eyes. *If he could have disappeared into the fruit bowl he would have,* thought Murdoch. The judge scowled.

"This is very presumptuous, sir. What is your business?"

"I wouldn't dream of interrupting at such an important time, except that I'm investigating a serious case, your honour."

"Yes, what is it?"

Murdoch hesitated ostentatiously. Let them sweat.

"I'm particularly here to talk to Mrs. Pedlow."

"My wife! I don't understand. Why would you want to talk to my wife?"

Maud had obviously not told her husband about Murdoch's previous visit. Burns fiddled with the dishes on the sideboard, waiting to hear what was going on. Mrs. Pedlow regarded Murdoch the way Macbeth might have stared at Banquo's ghost.

"Madam, did you not inform his honour of my interview?"

She shook her head and dabbed at her mouth with one of the damask napkins.

"No, of course not. It could have no relevance to him."

She stood up so quickly she jolted the table. Walter's coffee splashed out of the cup.

"Mrs. Pedlow, if you please!"

"I'm sorry, Walter. I think it would be better if Mr. Murdoch and I met in another room. We don't want to interfere with your tea."

The judge was not entirely a fool. He regarded her curiously. "Please sit down, my dear. If one of our police officers deems it necessary to come to my own house on official business I'd like to know what it is. Consider my position," he added ambiguously.

Maud sank back into her seat. Henry Pedlow was sitting very still and neither he nor his aunt looked at each other. Walter wiped off most of the cream custard from his mouth and decided to be gracious.

"I can spare some time, Mr. – er – Merton. Fortunately we

are having a cold meal today."

"I'm glad of that, sir."

Pedlow glanced up sharply but Murdoch had kept his face expressionless.

"Burns, bring Mr. Murdoch a chair," said Maud.

The butler pulled a cane-back chair closer to the table. Murdoch placed his hat beside him on the floor and took out his notebook with some deliberation. Anything to intimidate these people.

"Bear with us, Henry, this won't take long," Pedlow said.

For the second time that day, Murdoch felt a surge of anger and the muscles in his neck tightened. The condescension in the judge's voice infuriated him. Pedlow might as well have been talking about a pauper begging for alms.

"I can't promise that, sir," he said. "I must take all the time necessary. I am investigating two murders."

"Two? What do you mean?" Maud gasped.

"Hold on, Mrs. Pedlow," said her husband. "I don't even know about one. Start at the beginning, Merton, if you please."

He waved at him to begin as if he were a lawyer at the bench. Murdoch flipped over a few pages in his notebook, trying to get back his own control. No sense in letting a blowfly like Pedlow get under his skin. He could also feel how intently Henry Pedlow was paying attention and it aggravated him. His honour hadn't deemed it necessary to introduce his nephew to a detective so Henry was saved the embarrassment of having to admit a prior acquaintance. Murdoch didn't insist, deciding to keep that particular ace up his sleeve for now. Close up, the younger Pedlow wasn't as attractive as he'd first seemed on the stage with Annie. Even the brown skin couldn't mask the deep shadows underneath his eyes. Murdoch had an uncharitable feeling of satisfaction.

"Well? Get on with it," said the judge.

"A few days ago, I spoke to Mrs. Pedlow concerning the unnatural death of a woman named Dolly Shaw –"

"Why would my wife know anything of such a person?"

"Her daughter takes in washing," murmured Maud.

Murdoch saw no reason he should spare her. "I discovered Mrs. Pedlow's card in the dead woman's desk. There was also a copy of a letter that could be construed as a blackmail threat."

"How so?"

"The note mentioned previous services rendered which would be revealed unless a gratuity, her word, was tendered."

"Addressed to whom?"

"I don't know, sir, there was no name."

"And you say a copy. Am I to take that to mean you do not have the original?"

"That is correct, sir."

"Therefore, not only do you not know for whom this letter was intended, you do not know if it was actually sent, or when."

"You are right on all counts, sir."

"Aha." The judge sat back with the tips of his fingers forming a tent.

"I also found a large sum of money on the woman's person."

"How large?"

"Five hundred dollars. Ten fifty-dollar bills."

"You are, therefore, of the opinion she may have received these monies from her intended mark."

"It seems likely."

"But you have no proof."

"Not at the moment. One of the neighbours says that Mrs. Shaw used to be a midwife and she boasted about an album she had in which she kept her records. Records of sin, as she referred to them. I'm assuming, of course, she dealt with babies conceived out of wedlock. So far I have not found this book."

"I see. You're trying to make a tidy package of everything, aren't you? Threatening letter, money, some kind of records. Your thinking is rather acute, I'll give you that, Merton. Except I don't know where some poor wretch of a shop clerk would get the amount of money you found."

"Doesn't have to be a shop girl, sir."

The judge considered his wife. "Were you acquainted with this woman, my dear?" He was now totally in his element. He'd reverted to the kindly judge demeanour.

"Of course not."

Henry spoke for the first time. "Really, Uncle, how could she be?"

Pedlow ignored him, but Murdoch knew that both of them, detective and judge, had registered the intensity of Henry Pedlow's intervention.

"How did the woman come by your card?" Walter asked his wife.

"I don't know, I truly don't. One of the servants stole it probably. When I was visiting somebody. Passed it on to her."

"For what purpose?"

"Please, Walter, you are making me feel as if I'm on the witness stand." Maud tried unsuccessfully to laugh.

"Uncle! I must add my protest. We are not in court. My poor aunt is about to melt in a puddle in the heat of all these questions."

Henry was right about Maud's state and Pedlow frowned. "I am so sorry, my dear, I got quite carried away." He settled a pince-nez on his nose and glared at Murdoch. "Do you see what happens when decent people are intruded upon in this manner?"

"My apologies, Mrs. Pedlow."

"*You* are only doing your duty, sir."

The implied reproach was not lost on her husband and it seemed to incite him the way fear in a mouse will incite a terrier. He pounced.

"Am I to understand, Mrs. Pedlow, that you have received no begging letter or threatening letter from this woman?"

"No, of course not."

He turned to Murdoch. "You said Mrs. Pedlow's visiting card was the only one you found on the woman's premises?"

"That's right."

"How did the wretched woman die?"

"She was suffocated, sir. With a pillow from her couch. It is possible she was then dragged to the hearth and her head was banged against the fender."

"I see. So we are most likely looking for a person with

physical strength, a man no doubt."

"I wish I could be that definite, your honour. As I said, it is possible this is what happened. The physician couldn't in fact say when the blow to her head had occurred. Mrs. Shaw may have fallen on the fender before she was suffocated and her murderer took advantage of the moment."

Pedlow sniffed, aware he'd fallen into some kind of trap.

"Let us rest this case for a moment. You said there were two deaths?"

"Yesterday evening the body of Mrs. Shaw's foster son George Tucker was found stabbed to death."

"But he's a boy…"

"So he is, ma'am."

"Was he a boy?" the judge asked.

"He was twelve or thirteen."

"Any suspects?"

"Not exactly. Dolly Shaw's daughter, a grown woman, has run off and there is another foster child, who has also disappeared."

"Sounds like they're your culprits," interjected Henry. "Partners in crime."

Once again Murdoch was struck by how rigid the man was. He was sitting forward in his chair as if he had a stick up his backside.

"Let's not jump to conclusions, Henry. If Mr. Merton was sure of that, it's not likely he'd be here trespassing on our teatime is it?"

"That's correct, your honour. We haven't arrested anybody yet. But this morning, I made another search of the house and

I found this piece of newspaper."

He took it out of his pocket and handed it to Maud. "As you can see, ma'am, it is a photograph of your nephew's recent reception."

Quick as a snake, Walter intercepted the paper. "What do you think is the significance of that, Merton?"

"My name's Murdoch, sir. Acting Detective William Murdoch. And I was hoping Mrs. Pedlow might be able to enlighten me."

Maud's hand was fluttering around her cheek. "I'm afraid not. It's most strange."

"Well, at the risk of my uncle reprimanding me for hasty conclusions," interjected Henry, "I'd say you already have two good suspects. Who knows why they bothered to save this photograph?" He smiled. "I didn't realize I was so celebrious. But truly, Officer, why would the daughter disappear unless she had a guilty conscience?"

Walter couldn't resist the opportunity.

"You wouldn't have made a good lawyer, Henry. Never assume. There are many reasons the woman might have run off. Fear for one. I've known many an innocent party act so guilty they might as well have placed the rope around their own necks. All from fear."

There was something about the way he said the word that turned Murdoch's stomach. Relish. An almost lascivious delight in his own power and the helplessness of the victims. He turned his attention back to Maud.

"I take it you can't help with this matter, ma'am? You have never met the boy, George, or his foster brother?"

"Objection, Murdoch. She has already said she did not know the woman so she is not likely to have met the boys."

"With respect, your honour, the one does not necessarily preclude the other."

"Got you there, Uncle." Henry Pedlow was still trying rather desperately to inject a note of levity into the situation. Pedlow frowned at his wife. The kindly judge demeanour had vanished like a winter sunshine.

"Come now, answer his question, Mrs. Pedlow. Did you ever meet a boy named George... what?"

"George Tucker, your honour," Murdoch answered. "The other boy is named Alfred Locke."

"No. Never. Not at all... I'm sorry."

"You don't know of them, do you, sir?" asked Murdoch.

"Have they been up in front of my bench do you mean?"

"That as well."

"No, can't recall. But I will ask my clerk to check the records. This is most unpleasant. Perhaps this woman Dolly Shaw was planning to harm me. You never know how warped some people's minds can get if they feel they have suffered an injustice. The daughter is at large and might be insane for all we know."

Pedlow looked worried and Murdoch wondered if he'd received threats before. He wouldn't be surprised, given his notoriously harsh sentences.

"I want you to pursue this vigorously, Murdoch."

"I have every intention, sir."

Pedlow scrutinized him. "Have we met before? Have you ever been before my bench?"

"Yes, I have. I was a witness in the Jimmy Mashuter case."

"I don't recall…"

"He stole some gloves. It was wintertime and he had frostbite in four fingers. He was a child of the streets, no parents worthy of the name. You sent him to the penitentiary for three years."

Pedlow flapped his hand in Murdoch's direction. "I detect criticism in your voice, Mr. Murdoch, but in all my years on the bench I have been steadfastly of the opinion that firm measures in the beginning will save the criminal and society itself later transgressions."

"The boy was placed among hardened criminals, sir. He hanged himself shortly after he arrived at the prison."

Pedlow shrugged. "Obviously of a weak character. Wouldn't have amounted to much." He reached over and patted his wife's hand. "Now don't think too harshly of me, Mrs. Pedlow. These are the difficult decisions I face every day. You have no idea how burdensome they feel sometimes."

Murdoch stood up abruptly. "Thank you for your time."

Pedlow snapped his fingers at the butler, who had been watching the proceedings with frank curiosity.

"Burns, see Mr. Murdoch out if you please."

As he stood up, Murdoch addressed Henry Pedlow. "We've met before, I believe, sir."

"Where?" asked his uncle.

Henry contrived to appear embarrassed. "In truth it was at a tavern, was it not, Mr. Murdoch?"

"Why didn't you say so?"

"It didn't seem necessary, Uncle."

"What tavern?"

"I don't recall. I sometimes enjoy rubbing shoulders with the working classes. Gives me a perspective on life, as it were."

Walter considered him, clearly not conned. However, he chose not to pursue the matter. Murdoch saw the decision and knew it was not made from affection or concern for Henry. He wouldn't invite the possibility of shit being revealed in front of the detective. Murdoch felt a decidedly unchristian desire for the entire Pedlow family to be humbled. He was actually contemplating ways and means when he realized Pedlow was talking to him.

"I'm sure the malefactor will appear in front of me before long, eh, Murdoch? We'll throw the book at him."

"Perhaps the circumstances will dictate that, sir. And we don't know for sure. The malefactor might be a woman. And that changes everything, doesn't it?"

Surprisingly Pedlow didn't take offence.

"Not in my court it doesn't. Doesn't matter to me what's under their clothes. Pegs or holes, makes no difference."

CHAPTER TWENTY

THE BATHROOM AT THE YEOMAN CLUB WAS LUXURIOUSLY appointed. The water closet was of mahogany and porcelain, the faucets solid brass, the towels of satin damask. Annie, mother naked, was washing herself out with a rubber douche. Fenton was most particular about using French letters, but tonight he'd been too full, too lazy to use one. In fact, Annie had manoeuvred this state of affairs, pretending an urgency of desire she did not at all feel. She had her scheme well planned and it needed to be plausible. In two or three weeks she would approach him with anxious sighs, a tear unbidden. Then a little later, a frightened confirmation. If necessary she was quite prepared to escalate to hysterical scenes. She knew there was no chance of Fenton marrying her. He was a man of high aspirations. Next year he intended to run for alderman, and however cunt-struck he might be presently she doubted he could be pushed into such an unsuitable marriage. She'd read in the *News* that he had been paying court to the young daughter of one of his partners. So much the better. More reason for him to want Annie's silence. Besides, she didn't really want to marry. Not yet. In spite of the vulgarity of the Derby she liked the life, the attention, the feeling she had on good nights that she held them captive. Even the drunkest sot was silent when she sang "Home Sweet Home".

She winced at the cool water. No, a handsome settlement for pain and suffering would be enough. She'd slip out of Fenton's life, let him know discreetly that their problem had been solved and put the money away. She'd played out this script twice already with different men.

Annie finished what she was doing, put the douche back in its case, and started to get dressed. She studied herself in the mirror and frowned at her reflection. *I'm getting as bad as Millie. Can't lose my looks just yet.* She pinched her cheeks to make them glow. She pulled a face at herself, a bit saucy but innocent. Promise of fun, naughty fun. A little lowering of the chin, raising of her eyes, they all liked that. When you give me your look, said Fenton, I grow erect at once.

She got sick of them sometimes. The knee tremblers, the flyers, the back scuttlers. All for what? Less than a minute's worth of tickle and sneeze. But her savings in the Dominion

Bank on King Street were growing. When she had enough money she intended to buy her own business and then she could afford to pick and choose her own man, if she wanted one at all. She'd even look after Millie and her brat if Meredith got stubborn.

She breathed in and hooked up her corset. Her dress smelled of sweat and cigar smoke. She would have liked to have worn fresh clothes but she'd come directly from the Derby to the rendezvous with Fenton, who was presently snoring and snuffling in the bed. He'd been too drunk to remember to leave money but she had no compunction about dipping into the pocket of his trousers where he'd stuffed his bill folder. She took out two ten-dollar bills and put them into her chatelaine, snapping it closed with more anger than she realized. There was no sound outside in the hall. Everybody was asleep, the waiters gone. Tonight she was glad to be leaving so late. She felt as if her nerves were at the surface of her skin, and the contemptuous glances she usually elicited would burn.

Millie pushed the quilt off her legs. Her pregnancy made her hot all the time. She was half asleep, uncomfortable with the heartburn she had suffered from for the last week. She heard the front door open softly and a light tread across the threshold. Quickly, she turned to face the wall, not wanting Annie to know she was awake. Her sister was often full when she came in, and she stank of cigars and another smell that Millie didn't want to identify. Better not to be awake.

Last night, she'd denied her sister, ignoring the whispered plea. "Millie, are you asleep? Millie?"

Annie was quite capable of shaking her roughly awake if she wanted to and this soft, plaintive whisper frightened her more than any anger could have. But she hadn't responded and Annie had gone into the kitchen, where she had started to cry. *Why was she mithering*, thought Millie resentfully. *She wasn't the one with her apron up.*

The floorboard creaked again. Annie was being uncommonly quiet. Probably so sozzled she couldn't walk straight. Again a footstep. She suddenly smelled something pungent. She started to turn. "Annie, what –"

A knee was pressed against her back forcing her into the bed. One hand pushed her head into the pillow, the other jammed a cloth against her nose and mouth. There was something on the cloth, sickeningly sweet but stinging at the same time. It invaded her nose and throat, choking her. She couldn't move from the weight pinning her down, couldn't scream, couldn't breathe.

Dark red clouds wrapped around her, pulling her downward, paralyzing her limbs so she could no longer struggle, only sink into a fast-moving river of unconsciousness.

CHAPTER TWENTY-ONE

IN A SUDDEN CHANGE OF WEATHER, FRIDAY WAS WET AND cool. Murdoch was still feeling chilled from his damp morning ride and downing two mugs of enamel-destroying tea hadn't helped that much. The grey light, the patter of the rain on the window, the memories that had been stirred yesterday were lowering his spirits. Usually, the worn furniture in his cubicle was comfortably familiar but this morning it looked shabby and second-rate. He was glad when he heard Crabtree's solid tread in the hall. The constable stepped into the cubicle.

"There's a telephone call for you, sir. A Mr. Bright. Says he's a druggist."

Murdoch jumped up and followed him back to the main room of the station where the telephone was situated. The young duty officer glanced at him curiously. Telephone calls were few and far between.

"Murdoch here."

Mr. Bright wasn't used to his new instrument yet, and he spoke at top volume.

"I did some tests on those pills you gave me... Can you hear me?"

"Indeed I can, sir. In fact, you can speak a little softer if you like."

"Oh, right! The wife says I bellow into this dratted thing." He obviously moved further away from the mouthpiece because Murdoch could now hardly make out what he was saying. "How's that?"

"Somewhere in the middle would be perfect, sir."

This time he got it right but began to speak in a slower than normal voice. "Nothing in there that shouldn't be. Iron from the beef blood, some wheat for filler. They won't hurt you any if you take them in moderation."

"And if you don't? Take them in moderation, I mean?"

The druggist chuckled. "They won't kill you but they'll bind you up something terrible. You won't be able to pass out a pea. They'll likely give you bad piles too."

"I see. Thank you, Mr. Bright. I appreciate your help."

"Not at all. Just take two tablespoons of fig syrup oil morning and night 'til you're regular."

Murdoch realized the druggist thought the pills belonged to him and that he was too embarrassed to admit to it.

They hung up. Crabtree was standing at the counter that divided the room. Murdoch was aware suddenly that the big man seemed to take every opportunity to remain standing. He walked over to him.

"Crabtree, a word in your ear."

He whispered his question so none of the other constables could hear. Crabtree flushed but he nodded.

"Yes, sir. For almost two weeks."

Murdoch asked him another question and again he nodded, shamefaced.

"Quite painful if the truth be told, sir."

Murdoch passed on the druggist's recommendation.

"You can get the stuff at –"

Suddenly the outer door slammed open. The young woman who burst in was dressed in startlingly garish and indecorous clothes. A couple of old men who had come to complain about each other stared open-mouthed, and the constables at the duty desk lit up with excitement. Annie Brogan was in her stage costume.

She saw Murdoch and came over to him.

"I need to talk to you. In private." Her previously flirtatious manner had quite vanished and she seemed oblivious of the leering men.

"Of course. This way, please." He paused. Annie looked quite exhausted. "Can I get you a cup of tea?" he added.

A strange expression crossed her face and Murdoch didn't realize at first that she had forced back tears.

"Thank you. That's kind. I could do with one."

"I'll bring it in, sir," said Crabtree.

Murdoch ushered Annie through the passageway to his cubicle.

"You'll have to not mind my clothes. I haven't had a chance to change since I did my show."

"What's the matter?"

"I've been with my sister at the general hospital for the last eight hours." She bit her lip. "I thought I'd lost her."

They were interrupted by Crabtree with a mug of tea. She took it and managed a vestige of her old smile. She gulped some down.

"Ouch! It's hot." But she drank some more, greedily. Murdoch waited. She drained back the tea, wiping her mouth with the back of her hand. She'd rubbed away most of the colouring from her eyelids and she seemed more vulnerable, younger even.

"I'll get to the point. Last night, about one o'clock, somebody came into my house and drugged my sister, Mildred –"

"Drugged?"

"Chloroform. I didn't get home until almost two." She glanced away from him. "I was dining with a friend of mine. I keep late hours. Anyway when I came in, there was Millie half on the bed and half on the floor." She paused, struggling for self-control. "She was so white and still, I thought she was dead. Thanks be to God, she's not. I managed to get her sitting up and she started to come around."

In fact, Annie had stuck her fingers down Millie's throat until she vomited all over both of them.

"What happened?"

"She doesn't know. All she remembers is hearing somebody come into the room – thought it was me and didn't want to admit she was awake, nocky bint. Then this stinking cloth was over her face. It was chloroform for sure. She still reeked of it."

"Any idea who did it?"

"Could I have another cuppa char, Mr. Murdoch? I'm parched."

"I'll get you one in a minute." He knew she was stalling and he didn't want to lose her. "Is your sister all right now?"

Annie looked away again. "Yes. Millie wasn't forced or anything like that. She'll live."

"So who was it?" he repeated. "What did they want?"

"Who I don't know. Why is probably to take something of mine."

"What?"

She retreated, sipped the last of her tea, then came back to her resolve.

"A book. An album – this is the truth now and I don't care if it gets me into trouble. It was me your man saw going into Dolly's house the night she was stiffened – and I didn't do it so get that out of your mind."

"It wasn't in."

"Yes, well. You were right, I went there to get something for

Millie. I knew Dolly from before, and she would give you stuff like that. For a price of course. A high price."

"And did she?"

"Yes." She hesitated, trying to step on the stones and not in the quicksand. She intended to tell Murdoch only what suited her. "I bought what I came for, but she took out this autograph album. It was pretty, blue leather and gold letters. When her back was turned I nicked it."

"And somebody came to your house, almost killed your sister, and stole this book and nothing else?"

"Yes."

"Why? Why would they go to the trouble of chloroforming a woman for an album, however gold the letters? You can go to a fancy goods store on King Street and buy a dozen. You can order them from Sears catalogue. This is a bit extreme wouldn't you say?"

She shrugged. "People are mad as mice sometimes. I can't explain what's in the klep's mind."

"Annie, come on. This is horse plop, as you call it."

Annie began to play with a thread on her skirt. In another situation she would have turned it into something coy but now she just looked like a child trying to find a way out of trouble.

"Miss Brogan! Annie! Look at me! I'm real sorry for what happened to your sister, but I can't do anything about it unless you stop giving me the runaround. Besides, I happen to know what was special about that album."

"You do, do you?"

"Dolly Shaw told her neighbour that it was her record book. She called it a record of the sins of the world."

Annie scowled. "Did she now?"

"What was in it really?"

"I suppose you could call it that, I wouldn't. There's lots of girls get caught. And they're the ones who pay, not the gassers." Her voice was bitter. "Dolly Shaw never asked questions. She was a good midwife, mind you, but it was discretion you paid the muck for. And it's true. She did write everything in her sodding album. Names and dates. I saw her."

"When was that?"

"Doesn't matter. A long time ago."

"Did Dolly try to put the squeeze on you? Some dosh in exchange for silence?"

"You have to be pulling it. I'm already a Jezebel in the eyes of the world. Who'd care if there were more dilberries to be seen on my arse?"

"You are mentioned, though?"

"I didn't say so."

"Why'd you steal the book, then?"

"I had my reasons, but they don't concern you."

"They might."

"I wasn't planning to put the touch on the poor tits who fell into her clutches, if that's what you're worried about."

"I wasn't."

Annie stared at him, trying to read his expression, then she said, "All right. What else do you want to know?"

"Who knew the album was in your possession?"

"I don't know. My sister saw it but that's all."

"Was Dolly aware you'd nicked it?"

Annie laughed. "She wasn't dead yet. She had to know, seeing she was clutching it to her bosom when we had our dustup. I snatched it out from her."

"This is the truth now? You had a quarrel?"

"That's it."

"What about?"

"It's not relevant."

Murdoch let that go, trying to play the line gently.

"Somebody must have come soon after you left. Dolly might have told them you had the book."

"Hey, do I hear right? What you just said could be construed as a belief in my innocence."

"That's my assumption at the moment."

She grinned again. "When you come to the Derby and said she was dead, I thought I was the one as killed her. She fell down, you see, when I grabbed the book. She was drunk to her top knot. I could hear her moaning when I left so I was pretty certain she was still quick, but you gave me a heart-stopper for a minute. It was a great relief to me that the old sod was suffocated, God forgive me."

"Did she hit her head on the fender when she fell?"

"No. She sort of staggered backwards and sat on her behind against her desk. She wasn't near the hearth at all."

"How long were you in the house, would you say?"

"Not long. Must have been with her for half an hour at the most."

"Which way did you go when you left?"

"Straight down River Street. I picked up a cabbie on Queen Street. You can get his docket. Old guy, name of Aloysius. Horse was a dapple."

"What were you and Mrs. Shaw arguing about?"

"Nothing in particular. Dolly was very nasty when she had a skin on."

"How much did you pay for the abortifacient?"

She grimaced. "As it turned out, I didn't pay anything. We had the barney and I grabbed the album and ran, taking my money with me. She'd given me the herbs already. Wasn't stealing; she owed me."

"Miss Brogan, I found a copy of a letter in her desk that was asking for money. It wasn't addressed. Will you swear to me Dolly Shaw didn't send you that letter?"

"I swear. Besides, she wasn't so thick as to think she'd get much dosh from me."

Murdoch believed her but he wasn't going to let her off so easily just yet. He regarded her sombrely.

"It is obviously to your benefit if we find her murderer soon. Somebody is willing to take extraordinary risks to get the information in that book."

"Well, they've got what they want now."

"But this person must believe you have that knowledge as well. They might want to erase it. Make sure it dies with you."

"You'd better find them then."

"Come clean and give me a chance to."

Annie sat silently for what seemed like a long time. She glanced around at the cracked walls, the dingy chair, and filing cabinet. She waved away a persistent fly. Murdoch sat as patiently as he could. Finally, she said, "I want you to find who attacked Millie. She didn't deserve it… The chloroform caused her to miscarry."

Murdoch pulled out his handkerchief and gave it to her.

"It's funny," Annie continued. "You wish and pray that the thing inside you won't live, but when it doesn't, you feel very bad."

She blew her nose indelicately and rubbed at the tears. Looking very sad, she said, "If I tell you my own wicked story, are you certain it will be of help?"

"It might."

"Here goes then." She raised her hand in a mock toast. "When I was young and foolish." She smiled slightly. "We all do something foolish when we're young, don't we, Mr. Murdoch?"

"Certainly." He didn't consider her exactly old now but he didn't say anything.

"I had a lover. A wonderful, handsome prince. My Othello. I was only seventeen, and like Desdemona I loved him for the tales he told. He promised to marry me, the usual malarkey to get what he wanted. I got one in the oven pretty fast, and lo, my adoring lover wasn't quite so adoring. He'd neglected to mention a wife and family pining for him somewhere in America. He gave me enough money to get by, sent me off to Dolly's, and slipped away into the night. I went to lie in at her house in Markham, and on February the fourth, in the early hours of the morning, I was delivered of a baby boy." She stopped and tipped her empty cup, trying to find sustenance in it. "I was just starting on the stage and I couldn't raise a nipper on my own, so Dolly arranged for the baby to go to a farmer's family in the village. I only saw him once, never even held him in my arms. Dolly wouldn't let me." Unconsciously, she placed her hand at her bosom. "I had to promise I would make payments every month, two dollars for the child's maintenance. My baby wasn't easy to place, you see. Dolly said nobody would take him unless I agreed to pay regularly. Coming up with the muck was hard but I did it. Sent her money faithfully. For eight years. When I went to see her for Millie, I asked how the boy was doing. I'd been thinking for a long time that I'd like to visit him. Incognito of course – I didn't want to disturb his life, which I hoped was a happy one."

Annie stared into her teacup as if she could read her own fortune in the dregs. "I mentioned this to Dolly and asked her if I could have the name of the family that took him. She sneered at me. 'Oh dear,' said she. 'Didn't I tell you? He's dead and gone to heaven. Sickly little thing he was, didn't live out the winter.' Well that was a shocker, I tell you. 'What about the money?' I said. 'What money? You haven't been sending any money.' 'Yes, I have.' 'Prove it,' she said. 'There's no record.' I knew she wrote everything down in that album because I'd seen her do it when I was at the farm. She took it out of the desk and waved it under my nose. 'I owe you four dollars,' she said. 'I'll take it off your bill.'

"I was in a rage, Mr. Murdoch. That she'd cheated me for all these years. Once she'd even asked for extra because she said the boy had the measles and needed to see a doctor. I went without and sent the money. Always thinking I was helping. You see, I hoped one day he'd know that his... that his mother had cared. That I'd done my best. Dolly was chortling away. I screamed at her and snatched up the bloody album. I dunno, I wanted to see for myself if it was true. I wanted names." She twisted the handkerchief into a knot. "When I got home I was like a frigging green girl. I got all trembly, couldn't bear to open the shicey thing. I stuffed it in the drawer... and now I'll never know for sure if my boy is alive."

Murdoch felt compassion for her but he had to tighten the line, bring her in. He opened his file and showed her the calling card and the piece of newspaper.

"Tell me the truth, Annie. Was Mrs. Pedlow a customer of Dolly's?"

She took the card, staring at it. At the neat black script. The respectable name.

"That wasn't what she called herself then. She was known as Mrs. Brown. But she was there at the same time as me. She delivered two weeks before I did."

"What happened to her baby? Was it adopted?"

"Not as far as I know. But everything to do with Mrs. Brown was so hush-hush. There was a wetnurse came in from the village for a few days and Missus left soon after with her infant. A girl it was."

"There's a child living with her now but she's supposedly the Pedlows' ward."

Annie nodded. "I know. When I went up there, I asked her and she told me the first infant died."

"Do you believe her?"

"I don't know. Maybe it's true."

"She was a respectable married woman, why would she have to hide her pregnancy?"

"Come on, Mr. Murdoch. Don't be nocky. People can count, you know. Maybe her husband was away at an inconvenient time. Or maybe he couldn't get his pecker up. He'd know whether he was the baker or not."

"If he wasn't the father she'd have to make up some story as to why she had an infant in tow."

"That's it."

"Did Maud Pedlow know you'd been to see Dolly?"

"Yes, I told her."

Agitated, Annie stood up, although there was nowhere to pace in the tiny office. "I told her everything. Not about taking the album but what Dolly had said about my boy being dead. I needed to tell somebody. There wasn't anybody else to talk to. Even Millie doesn't know."

Murdoch hesitated, almost afraid of what he had to say.

"Annie, when I went to interview Mrs. Pedlow yesterday, I told her that Dolly's record book was missing. Her husband

and her nephew were both present."

"I see." Unexpectedly, she touched his arm. "Wasn't your fault. You didn't know. But it must have been one of them, or a messenger for one of them."

"Looks that way."

She slammed her fist on his desk.

"This cull, the nephew? The one who's been licking his chops around my diddies – is he the one who came after Millie?"

"It's possible."

"That's a big favour to do for your auntie. Almost murder somebody so she can sleep at night. You know what I think, Mr. Murdoch? I'm thinking the frigging nephew is the real baker. The one who stuck my lady high and mighty. She wouldn't want that little secret in the papers, would she?"

Murdoch remembered the scene at the Pedlows'. The intensity of Henry's response. He had the feeling Annie was right. And if Henry had chloroformed Millie, he might have gone for Dolly. Same reason.

"If it's true, would Dolly have known it?"

"She knew everything. Most of the girls lied, about being married mostly. Whenever one of them went into the village, she'd go through their belongings. I caught her red-handed one day. She didn't care. 'I have to protect myself,' she said. I'd bet my life she did the same for Missus."

Again Murdoch hesitated. She was eyeing him curiously.

"What's up?" she asked.

"Why did you say the child you bore was hard to place?"

"What?"

He repeated the question.

She looked defiant. "He wasn't deformed or sick or anything like that. I was clean."

"Why then?"

"Dolly hammered it home to me. Nobody's going to want this by-blow unless you pay. Then they might."

She raised her head and smiled. There was fondness in the smile. "His father was strong and handsome as ever you saw, but he was a coloured man."

Before she could continue, they heard Crabtree hurrying down the hall. He parted the reed strips.

"There's a lad out here, sir. Says he saw young Freddie going into the Shaw house."

"When?"

"Just now. He knew as we were looking for the laddie and he ran right here."

Murdoch pushed back his chair. "I've got to leave. Crabtree, go make sure the messenger doesn't escape."

Murdoch waited until the constable was out of earshot.

"Miss Brogan, I'd like you to come with me."

"Me? Why?"

"I don't want to raise false hopes but I believe Dolly was lying to you."

"How d'you mean?"

"There's a foster son who's been living with her. He's about eight years of age and he's part coloured."

She gasped and a look of such joy came into her face that he could have wept.

"Do you want to come with me? If he is your son, he needs your help bad."

All she could do was to nod her agreement.

CHAPTER TWENTY-TWO

A GANGLY YOUTH WAS OUT IN THE PUBLIC AREA. HE WAS wearing a tight navy sweater and check bicycle trousers, nipped at the knee. A scorcher if ever there was one. His face was streaked with rain, and he smelled of damp wool.

"You told the constable you've seen the boy we're looking for. Tell me," said Murdoch but Annie Brogan was at his elbow and, seeing her, the young man looked as if he wasn't going to utter words again.

"What's your name, son?" Murdoch asked him.

"Jim McEvoy, Junior, sir. I live at number one-twenty-eight, just down the road from Mrs. Shaw." He paused. "Er, the late Mrs. Shaw that is – you know the one who –"

"Yes, I know. Pay attention to the business at hand, Mr. McEvoy. Where did you see him?"

"He was sneaking into his house. I was out on my wheel. I deliver things about town, you see, sir. They've got a bit of a garden out back. For a minute I thought it was a lost dog or something like that, 'cos he was creeping close to the fence. I took a study because if it was there, might be a reward involved –"

"Get on with it, lad, you're trying my patience."

The youth flushed and Murdoch felt sorry he'd been so abrupt with him.

"When I realized it was Fred I just jumped on my wheel and came here as fast as I could."

Murdoch turned to the constable.

"Crabtree, I'm going right over there. I'll use my bicycle. Miss Brogan is coming too. Bring her along with you."

Annie caught hold of Murdoch's sleeve. "Please! I must get there as fast as I can. Let me come with you."

Her boots were of soft kid with a needle toe and higher heel. They didn't look the best footwear for a hurried walk but he understood her urgency.

"Can you ride a bicycle?" he asked.

"Yes. I've used one in my act."

Murdoch turned to the youth. "McEvoy, I've just requisitioned your wheel in the service of the police."

The boy blushed with delight. "My pleasure, sir, er, madam."

"You can come with the constable. Miss Brogan, let's scorch."

Annie, not caring, folded her skirts up and tucked them into her belt. She handled the wheel like a professional, and they got to the Shaw house in minutes. Fortunately, no curiosity had yet been excited and the street was deserted. Murdoch was praying that Freddie hadn't been alarmed and fled again. He signalled to Annie to dismount at the opposite corner. The rain was glistening on the macadam, sleeting through the drooping leaves of the trees.

"Do you mind the wet?"

She shook her head. She would have stood in fire and brimstone if necessary.

"It'd be better if you wait here, then. I'm going in the back way and you'll be able to see if he shoots out the front. If he does, grab him and yell for me. He's a little titch. You can hold on to him if you have to."

She nodded and he knew that she would risk her life at this point if she had to.

He crossed the road and walked casually in front of the house. There was no sign of anyone stirring; the curtains in the front parlour were still drawn tight. He went through the gate and walked around to the rear garden. The plot was given over to vegetables and well tended. Tomatoes were ripening on the vine, and there were several rows of potatoes and turnips. In the sunlight, the garden would have appeared lush and fertile; now it seemed desolate, the colour washed out by the rain.

When he had finished searching the house previously, he'd barred the back door from the inside and locked the front. Freddie had been forced to climb through the kitchen window. He'd trampled in the earth. The sash was pushed up and the sill muddy.

Murdoch leaned his head in first, cautiously. The window opened directly into the kitchen, where George had died. Murdoch stood still, trying to determine if he could detect the boy's presence, but the house remained quiet, as if it were holding its breath. He put his leg over the sill, scrunched his body, and slithered with some difficulty into the kitchen. Here he waited again. Nothing, except now he could hear the tick of a clock on the mantel. The heel of the loaf of bread was green with mould, and on the floor was a half-eaten unripe tomato. The cupboard door had swung wide open and he wondered if Freddie had come here in search of food.

He walked through into the hall.

"Hello! Anybody here? Freddie? It's Detective Murdoch. I'm not going to hurt you. Just come out. We've got to have a talk." Silence.

He could see the door to the parlour was open. He went to investigate but that room was also empty.

He returned to the hall, which was uncarpeted, and thumped his feet a couple of times as if he were walking. He closed the creaky door to the kitchen with a bang. Then he lowered himself to the floor and leaned against the wall. When he'd gone into the fields as a boy, he'd found the best way to see the wild deer or rabbits was to sit still and wait. He hoped Crabtree hadn't arrived yet and that Annie could hold out.

He'd been sitting for almost ten minutes when he was rewarded by a tiny sound, just the merest scrabble. Murdoch didn't stir. The noise had come from down the hall and he saw there was a cupboard underneath the stairs, the door open the slightest crack. He heard the scratching sound again but it lasted longer this time. The cupboard door shifted an inch wider and Freddie's dirty face appeared.

At first he didn't see Murdoch because of the gloom in the hall and he came out, crawling on all fours. At that instant the front door opened and Annie Brogan entered. Murdoch could see Crabtree standing behind her.

Freddie saw them all, whimpered, and made a dash for the stairs. Murdoch jumped up.

"Freddie, stop! Freddie!"

He charged after the boy and got to the top of the stairs as the boy raced into the bedroom on the left, slamming the door behind him. Annie also ran up the stairs. She halted on the landing. "I had to come in," she gasped. "I couldn't bear the wait any longer."

"Stay there," he said and slowly opened the door. For a moment it seemed as if the boy had vanished into thin air. The tiny bare room seemed completely empty. Murdoch held his breath to listen, but Freddie was unable to control his own panting. He was under the bed. Murdoch crouched down and found himself staring into one of the most terrified faces he had ever seen.

He got low to the floor and lay on his side, propped on his

elbow, the way he had when he'd watched a fox's den.

"Don't be afraid, lad. I'm here to help you."

Freddie shrank back further against the wall. Suddenly there was a scuffling sound and Annie plunged to the floor as well, not caring about dirtying her dress or the inelegance of her position. She peered at the boy, winced, and said softly, very softly, "My God, it is him. He's the spitting image." She almost broke into a sob but she held it back. "Freddie, please come out. I'm Annie Brogan and I do believe we've met before, a long time ago."

Murdoch was sitting on the chair by the door, while Annie, lying on her side, talked to Freddie. Her tone was as casual as if they were across a tablecloth at a picnic, although the boy was clad in only his nightshirt. Annie's dress was dark from the rain and her hair was bedraggled and falling down at her neck.

"You must be starving," she said. "I know what that's like. I used to be hungry a lot when I was a nipper. Do you want to come out and we'll get some good grub?" No answer. "I wouldn't mind some sausages and mash. I know a nice eating house just down on Queen Street. Not too far away. What d'you say?" Silence. Murdoch began to wonder if they were going to have to drag him out. Then he remembered the Cupid's Whispers he'd bought from Mr. Bright. He fished the tin out of his inside pocket, removed the lid, crouched down, and held them out to Annie. They were dipped in powdered sugar and smelled pleasantly fruity.

"Want one?"

She glanced at him in surprise, realized what he was doing, and smiled in delight.

"Sure would." She popped one in her mouth and made a great show of enjoying it, licking her lips. Murdoch took one himself, got down to floor level and held out the tin to Freddie. "Would you like one?"

Annie made more tasting sounds. "Can I have another?"

She took one. Murdoch waited. Then he put the tin on the floor and pushed it towards Freddie. He could see the boy's wide staring eyes, how thin his face had become. Suddenly, Freddie grabbed a handful of the lozenges and stuffed them in his mouth. There wasn't going to be a problem with unpleasant breath among any of them. The air beneath the bed was fragrant with the smell of raspberries.

"I know you're frightened, lad," said Murdoch. "But I promise we'll listen to your story fair and square. If you haven't done anything bad you won't be punished."

He saw the boy blink away a rush of tears. Then Freddie looked at Annie and said in a whisper, "What you mean you met me before?"

Annie slid further along the floor and stretched herself out. "I'm getting such a crick in my neck. Tell you what. If you come out from under there and sit on a chair beside me, I'll explain. And it's absolutely true what I said, on my honour. You look just like your father. And him and me knew each other well."

It was clear that Freddie was figuring it out. "Mrs. Mother said my real ma died from drink. She was a tart."

Annie swallowed hard. "She was lying, Freddie. On both counts. Listen, do you want to put your trousers on?"

He nodded and she got stiffly to her feet, grabbed the trousers, and pushed them towards the boy.

"I'm going to sit in this chair."

Murdoch stood up too and leaned against the door frame, ready to catch Freddie if he bolted. He sucked loudly on his lozenge. There was a scrambling sound from underneath the bed as Freddie struggled to dress. Then there was a tentative scratching noise and the boy's head emerged. He looked so worn and afraid that Murdoch wanted nothing more than to scoop him up and embrace him. However, he didn't move and neither did Annie. The boy squeezed himself out from under the bed but remained on all fours ready to scurry back at the first sign of trouble.

"Let's go down to the kitchen," said Murdoch. "I'll send Constable Crabtree off for some of those sausages and we can all have a talk."

Mutely, Freddie shook his head and looked as if he was about to retreat again. Quickly, Murdoch moved over, squatted down, and grasped hold of the boy's shoulder.

"You don't have any choice, lad."

Again Freddie shook his head. Annie spoke up.

"What I'm thinking, Mr. Murdoch, is that this house is a bad place to ask questions in. Is there anywhere else we can go to?"

Murdoch winced. Of course she was right. How could Freddie possibly sit in the kitchen where in all likelihood he'd last seen George bleeding away his life's blood.

"I think that's an excellent suggestion, Miss Brogan. Let's go across the road to that nice neighbour lady. See if she'd let us use her front parlour. Does that suit you, Freddie?"

He nodded. Murdoch hoped Mrs. Golding was still willing to be a Good Samaritan.

Annie held out her hand, and hesitantly Freddie took it. His head was lowered, every muscle poised ready to flee. Murdoch led the way out of the bedroom and onto the landing. Crabtree was standing at the bottom of the stairs but he didn't speak. Freddie stopped in his tracks when he saw the uniform but Murdoch didn't give him a chance to run away. Calmly, he said to Crabtree, "Just go across to Mrs. Golding's, will you, Constable. Tell her we're coming over. There's three of us."

"Yes, sir."

At the bottom of the stairs they had to go past the kitchen, but Annie made sure she was between Freddie and the door and she kept on walking, holding his hand firmly in hers.

Three things stood out for Murdoch about the next hour. First was how politely Mrs. Golding hid her astonishment at the sight of Annie Brogan. Second was watching Freddie gulp down the cold roast beef and bread like a starving dog. Almost immediately, he vomited it back all over the Goldings' best parlour rug. Mrs. Golding didn't make a murmur of reproach and on Annie's recommendation went to warm up some milk. The third memorable thing was Freddie's reaction to Murdoch's question.

"What happened, young lad? Who was it did in George? Can you tell me?"

Freddie was sitting close to Annie and he shuddered, put his head back, and wailed.

CHAPTER TWENTY-THREE

ONCE AGAIN, LILY HAD FLED TO HER HIDING PLACE in the riverbank. Her dress had been splattered with George's blood. Panting, she'd pulled off the garment, tearing the shoulder seam in her haste, and immersed it in the cool water. In the darkness, the stains were difficult to see, but she rubbed at them as best she could, over and over until her knuckles were raw and skinned. Finally she draped the dress on the branches to dry and crept into the cave. She was clad only in her chemise and drawers and she couldn't stop the violent shivering. She curled up as tightly as she could and sat at the entrance, rocking back and forth. When the sun finally rose and brought a blessed warmth to the air, she stayed there, crying, but keeping the cries close to her.

She had returned to the house, circling back to what was familiar. She had entered through the back door into the kitchen, suddenly ravenous, searching for food. Saliva had filled her mouth and dribbled down the corner of her lips. There was a bag of buns on the table and she ate two immediately, almost choking on the dry, stale pastry. She sawed off a piece of bread from the loaf that the boys had left and chewed at the end of a piece of cheese. She had moved as carefully as she could but, without knowing it, she banged the pots on the stove as she looked for more food. The boys had awakened and George, with Freddie behind him, came down to the kitchen. He laughed when he saw her and immediately started to mock her, to jeer at her hunger. "You're going to get it," he mimed. "They're going to throw you in jail for killing your mother. They're looking for you. You're in for it this time."

He pretended to put a rope around his neck, pull it tight, and dropped his head to one side, broken. "And your shit comes out," he said. He lifted his nightshirt and showed her how that happened, laughing all the time. Freddie had crouched in the corner of the room and he watched, frozen in dread, unable to help.

Perhaps none of that would have provoked her to murder, although she was so frightened. She would just have run away again. However, George knew what had happened before with the kidnapped baby, and eager for more cruelty he turned to that. He stuck his fingers in his mouth, pulling back his lips so they glistened raw and red. He held up his hand, the fingers glued together. He rocked the baby in his arms, making soothing gestures, but it was done to belittle her tenderness, to mock her love for the infant girl. Delighted at the reaction he had evoked in Lily, he pointed at her, cackling, tugging again at his mouth.

Then, sated in his fun, he turned to the cupboard, intending to get himself a mug or plate.

She seized the bread knife, ran around the table, and stabbed him. Once, twice, and again, while the hot blood shot out in an arc, drenching her.

She had lost any sense of how long she had been by the river. The way she had when she was in prison, she had taken herself into a trance, not moving, taking refuge in a world where she wasn't cold, where her mother and George were still alive, and where she was holding the baby again, caressing it, basking in the perfect smiles, the flawless hands.

She might have stayed there until she was discovered, but on the third morning a heavy rain began to fall, pocking the river, penetrating the opening of her den. Finally, not even Lily could withstand the discomfort and cold. She uncurled herself. The pain in her limbs as the blood flowed again was excruciating. She had to stand up. She eased herself out of the cave and reluctantly stretched her arms. There was no colour in the world. The sky, the trees, the river were all leached of brightness. The rain was hitting her face and bare shoulders and arms, cold and punishing. She shook her head, trying to get away but she couldn't. Close by was her dress. It was as soaked as the ground, but it offered some comfort. She reached for it and as she did, the soft, muddy earth gave way and she slipped. Unable to gain her balance she fell into the deep pool where the river was dammed. Her wide drawers twisted around her legs. Momentarily a primitive panic seized her, an instinct for life. She gasped for air but she swallowed water instead. Choking, she drew it up her nose, down her throat, into her lungs. She thrashed frantically but to no avail. The river was overpowering her. Perhaps another person would have fought harder, been able to free herself. Lily's struggles were soon only half-hearted. She had so little to come back to life for.

CHAPTER TWENTY-FOUR

MURDOCH DIDN'T BOTHER WITH EVEN RUDIMENTARY politeness when Burns opened the door.

"Where is Mrs. Pedlow? I have to see her immediately."

"She's in the drawing room, but –"

Murdoch pushed by him, leaving the butler spluttering a protest.

Maud was seated at the piano but he'd heard no music. She turned as he entered and he saw the fear jump into her eyes.

"Mr. Murdoch! I –"

"Mrs. Pedlow, I must speak to you."

"Please sit down."

"No, thank you, ma'am."

She stared at him. Her gown today was a plain grey silk with silver trims. The collar was white, stiff and high as a man's. The severity of the dress was not complementary to her pale skin and drab hair.

"Mrs. Pedlow, you have been less than honest with me."

She was about to object but the words wilted in the heat of his anger.

"I have spoken with Annie Brogan. She tells me you did know Dolly Shaw, or rather Dolly Merishaw –"

"That is not the –"

"Ma'am, according to Miss Brogan you were one of Dolly's customers eight years ago. She delivered you of a female child at her farm in Markham."

"How can you believe this woman, Mr. Murdoch? She is nothing but a common stage performer. She is trying to blacken my name."

Maud wouldn't have persuaded a cat.

"I have also been informed that Mrs. Shaw's foster son Freddie delivered a letter here on Thursday afternoon."

"I received no such letter."

"The boy swears he handed it to you personally. You wrote a letter in reply, which he gave to Mrs. Shaw."

She turned away from him, studying the sheet of music propped on the piano as if she were about to give a recital.

"Please answer me, ma'am."

Murdoch felt like grabbing her by the shoulders and spinning her around to face him.

"Mrs. Pedlow, I insist on your explanation."

At last she turned.

"Mr. Murdoch, I am certain there is not a person in the world who does not have some part of their lives they do not wish to expose to the world."

"Ma'am?"

"It is true, I did know the woman many years ago. I apologize for prevaricating but it was a most painful time for me. I preferred not to talk about it."

"You knew I was investigating a murder, yet you lied to me."

So much for fine vocabulary. He had the impulse to be obscene, rough-tongued. Anything to break through the woman's stubbornness.

"My involvement was so long ago, it seemed unimportant."

"That was for me to decide."

She was squeezing and rubbing at her hands as if she were warming up her fingers. She sighed ostentatiously.

"Very well. What you are so insistent on winkling out of me, Mr. Murdoch, is perhaps not such a terrible thing. It is, however, a delicate matter and I ask for your complete discretion."

"We'll see. I may have no choice in the matter."

Her little attempt at acting, which was laughable, fell away and when she spoke again, it was with more dignity.

"The fact is that rather late in my life, I conceived a child. My husband was away from home when I realized the happy news. I – I could not bear the scrutiny of my neighbours. I knew how they would gossip about a woman of my age being enceinte.

Perhaps I was too sensitive but I craved privacy. I saw Mrs. Merishaw's advertisement and went to her for my lying-in."

"And that's where you first met Annie Brogan?"

"I suppose it was, although to tell the truth there was more than one young woman at the farm and I did not care to associate with them."

"That must have been lonely for you, at such an important time?"

She shrank a little at that comment but still didn't crack. "Not at all. I am really quite a solitary sort of person, Mr. Murdoch."

"You told Miss Brogan your baby died shortly after birth."

"That is what I mean by a painful time of my life that I have no wish to relive. Fortunately, if I may put it that way, my cousin had given birth at almost exactly the same time as I, and the poor woman died in the childbed. Of course I wanted to adopt that little girl. To give her a decent home. My cousin was a widow, you see, and much impoverished by the entailment of her husband's estate. Taking on Sarah as my ward eased my terrible loss, as I am sure you can understand, Mr. Murdoch."

Murdoch thought he had never been conned by such an expensively dressed woman before.

"Your husband must have been grieved also."

Maud bent her head and spoke so quietly he could hardly hear her.

"My dear sir, I am in fact throwing myself on your mercy. You have asked me why I was trying to hide my acquaintance with Mrs. Merishaw. The truth is Mr. Pedlow does not know of my pregnancy. He has always longed for an heir and was dreadfully disappointed when it seemed as if God had seen fit not to so bless us. I decided to wait until the birth was assured before telling him. When the infant was taken from me, I saw no reason to inform him. I feared the sorrow would break his heart."

"I beg your pardon, Mrs. Pedlow. I find that incredible."

His sense of Pedlow's heart was that it would withstand the direct hit of a cannonball.

Her eyes fastened on his as she attempted to sound convincing. "I am telling you the truth. Walter is so delighted with Sarah. I have never told him about the other child and will not do so. As I said, Mr. Murdoch, I am throwing myself on your mercy. I have entrusted you with this painful secret. My future and the future of my little family is in your hands."

Murdoch shifted impatiently. "Does anybody else know?"

She smoothed her skirt, a gesture he had seen women use before when they were buying time.

"I confided in my nephew, Henry. Perhaps I shouldn't have, but my secret was sometimes a burden to me. He was very kind and allowed me my little weep and that was all I needed."

"Was Dolly Shaw aware that you had not told your husband about the child?"

"I don't see how she could have known one way or the other. We rarely talked. I had no further correspondence with her after I left Markham."

"There will be a record of the infant's death in the village register, I presume?"

"Mrs. Merishaw took care of all that. I was, er, too overcome."
And I suppose you could say that about Dolly now, he thought. She won't be able to confirm this story one way or the other.

"Do you now admit you received a letter from Mrs. Shaw which asked for money?"

"Yes, I did. I am sorry I did not tell you the truth at first. I..." Her voice tailed off, trying to lure him into gallantry.

"Did you answer it?"

"Yes. I felt sorry for the woman. I sent a few dollars with the boy."

Murdoch was recording all this information in his notebook. He took his time. Like Annie in the beginning, this woman was giving him only as much truth as she could get away with.

"Did your nephew know about Mrs. Shaw's letter?"

"I believe I did mention it to him, yes."

"What sort of person is Mr. Henry, would you say? Rash? Hot-tempered?"

"Not at all. He is most equable. Why do you ask, Mr. Murdoch?"

"I wonder if he might have taken it upon himself to seek out Mrs. Shaw. Just to make sure she was only asking for a small gratuity and not going in for a spot of blackmail. Is it likely he would have done something like that, Mrs. Pedlow?"

She was starting to look very tight about the mouth and jaw.

"I suppose it is not totally out of the question, but, Mr. Murdoch, I still don't see why you are pursuing this line of enquiry when surely you already have your culprit."

"Who is that, madam?"

"The unfortunate woman, Lily. Her mother treated her badly. I saw such on many an occasion. She must have finally retaliated. You said another boy was killed. It seems to me highly plausible that he was a witness to the first crime and the poor lunatic woman killed him also."

Murdoch now knew that wasn't what had happened, but he wasn't going to tell her yet.

"According to Freddie, Lily ran away before Mrs. Shaw was killed and did not return until the next day. I don't believe she murdered her own mother."

Maud gave a small shrug. "An intruder then –"

"Unlikely. The boy says he heard two people come to the house the night of the murder. Annie Brogan admits she was the first visitor, but she swears she left Dolly quite alive."

"Perhaps she is lying."

Maud was fickle in her choice of suspects.

"I don't think so. The person who came afterward is the one I'd like to talk to. Freddie couldn't tell if it was a man or a woman, but Mr. Golding heard somebody leaving the Shaw house about two o'clock in the morning. He had no doubt it was a woman he heard."

"In spite of what you say, we're back to the daughter then, aren't we? She's a husky woman."

Maud Pedlow was exhibiting more steel at the centre than he would have expected.

"Dolly Shaw was drunk. If she had fallen and knocked

herself senseless, it wouldn't take much physical strength to hold a pillow on her head, just great emotional resolve."

There was a long silence, more stiffening of the jaw, then Maud said, "If Dolly wrote a begging letter to me, I am sure she wrote to others. I was far from being her only client."

"The boy swears there was only one letter. She wrote it immediately after she saw the newspaper article about your nephew's reception."

"Mr. Murdoch, you are hounding me. I shall be forced to discuss the matter with my husband."

"In which case I would be forced to explain why I am asking you these questions, ma'am. You have good reason to want Dolly Shaw silenced."

"I find that an extremely impolite remark."

Murdoch almost laughed outright. "Politeness seems a little irrelevant in the case of murder, wouldn't you say, ma'am?"

Maud chose not to reply but she seemed more distressed. He pressed the advantage.

"To come back to Mr. Henry Pedlow for a moment. You say he is of an equable temperament? Is he a loyal person?"

"Yes, I suppose so."

"If he thought the happiness of you and your husband was at stake, might he lose that even disposition?"

"How can I answer such a question? However, I…"

"Please continue, ma'am."

Her voice was shaky when she replied. "I have been concerned about him. It is most upsetting to contemplate the implication of your question but –"

Again she faltered. Murdoch couldn't quite tell if he was in the presence of an actress of Sarah Bernhardt ability or if she was genuinely afraid of the possibilities.

"Why are you worried about your nephew?"

"He has shown signs of instability since returning from India, the sun –"

"Instability, ma'am?"

"Oh, I am sorry. I am not a physician. I shouldn't have said –"

"You don't need a medical degree to use the word. What do you mean by 'instability'?"

"He laughs at inappropriate moments, weeps at nothing... he has flown into terrible tempers over the smallest thwarting. A cabman who is too slow, a passerby who bumps him."

Murdoch regarded her. She was still seated at the piano and as she spoke, her shoulders drooped and her voice was flat. The arrogant veneer had disappeared.

"Do you think your loyal, unstable nephew is capable of murder?"

"If there is extreme provocation, who can ever know what a person is capable of, Mr. Murdoch."

She had avoided a direct answer but Murdoch got the message. She suspected Henry had killed Dolly and she was no doubt happy about it.

"Where would I find Mr. Pedlow now?"

"He is staying at the Avonmore Hotel. He said he had an important engagement this afternoon. I am certain he will be there!"

Murdoch went towards the door. He turned to take his leave.

Mrs. Pedlow was staring straight in front of her, and the expression on her face was one of utter anguish.

CHAPTER TWENTY-FIVE

HENRY PEDLOW HAD WOKEN EARLY BUT HE WAS STILL sitting in his pyjamas in the armchair beside the bed. A waiter had tapped on the door to deliver his breakfast but he'd sent him away with a surly command. Food seemed irrelevant to him. He was surprised when he came out of his reverie and saw it was after eleven o'clock. He had no recollection of what he had been thinking in the past four hours. He didn't believe he had fallen back to sleep, but the time had vanished, wiped away like a mark on the beach. Stiffly, he got to his feet. His limbs ached and his throat was on fire. The doctor had warned him, of course. It would get worse. A man of few words, he had only added, "We have morphine or opium for the pain, but in the end..." He shrugged. Henry hadn't known this physician long, only since he had arrived back in Toronto, and he knew the man disapproved of him, despised him for the disease. Not that Henry could blame him. He himself was filled with self-contempt. What a fool he'd been. What a stupid, stupid fool.

He began to pace, swept with a surge of emotion so violent he couldn't stand still. He slammed his fist down on the sideboard, making the ornaments bounce. *Stupid! Stupid! Fool!* He'd been warned as soon as he arrived in India. "Watch for the fireships. You can't always tell. Even the young ones can have it." But the soft, dark eyes, the compliance of the women proved irresistible.

As suddenly as it had come, his anger vanished. He burst into tears. He couldn't stop. Sobs racked his chest, hurting him, burning his throat. He finally forced himself to stop crying, not because the grief was over, but because the physical pain it created was too severe.

He was lying face down on the bed, his head buried in the pillows. He didn't remember moving there. Again he checked the clock. He had lost another half hour. Or had he? Was it ten past eleven when he had last looked? It was now almost noon.

Groaning, he got up off the bed. He'd asked for a fire to be laid and he walked over to the fireplace, struck a match, and lit the paper. The flames leaped, ready to lick around the coal. He waited for a moment but he was afraid to be still for long, too many thoughts rushed in. He went over to the escritoire by the window. The hotel provided stationery, rather good quality letter paper with the hotel crest at the top. He sat down, took one sheet, unscrewed the top of the inkwell, dipped in the pen, and wrote in large letters, "To Whom It May Concern."

He supposed he could address it directly to the detective who was investigating the case but he had forgotten his name.

She hadn't told him immediately, letting him meet Sarah and recounting the story she gave out to the world. This is my ward, and so on. It wasn't until she'd received the letter from Dolly Shaw that she told him the truth.

Henry's thoughts shied away, the shock of that revelation overwhelming him again.

He pulled up the window blind a few inches and gazed down onto the street. A carriage went by, the horse splashing in the rain-filled ruts. The driver, his waterproof glistening, flicked his whip and the horse broke into a canter. A man and a woman huddled together beneath a black umbrella as they hurried towards the hotel. He could see they were not young and something in the way they leaned in to each other, the closeness, suggested a conjugal familiarity

His envy was like the taste of bile on his tongue. He had never known such ease with any woman and would not now.

Except for Maud.

Their connection had meant little to him. A chance to take a willing woman, and he hadn't been in contact with her the entire time he'd been in India. Even her first dreadful revelation hadn't brought them closer. He'd felt guilt, fear, anger, but no real sympathy. Then she'd come to his hotel. She was frantic.

The police suspected her, she said. The detective was at her heels. She'd turned to Henry, as desperate as a deer at bay. Impatient with her fear and angry at what she'd done, he'd told her his own secret. He said it brutally, wanting to hurt her. She'd been jolted into agonized tears and then she'd reached for him and held him in her arms, her tears wetting his face. It was when he realized she was weeping for him and not just herself that Henry Pedlow experienced something approaching love for the first time in his life.

The memory was too painful to dwell on, and he looked out of the window again.

Across the road the lamps were lit in the houses. He could see into a drawing room, a maid straightening the antimacassars on the chairs ready for callers.

He felt himself move far away from the scene as if he were drawn up to a high mountain top. The carriage, the man and the woman, the houses, seemed like toys. Another sob threatened and he lowered the blind quickly.

"To Whom It May Concern.

"I wish to make a full confession to the murder." He crossed out the word, could think of none better, and rewrote it.

"the murder of Dolly Shaw."

He no longer knew who had first suggested this course of action, perhaps it was Maud. Regardless, he was now embracing it. In spite of human fear, his mind had become clear and precise. He continued.

"She had discovered details of my past life that I did not

wish the world to know. She was attempting to blackmail me. I went to her house to reason with her and in a moment of rage I killed her."

He paused. Was it necessary to elaborate? Better not. It was safer to keep it simple. However, he inserted, "By suffocation." He blotted the paper and concluded. "What I do here, I do in full possession of my faculties."

He considered adding, "I am a condemned man anyway," but he wasn't sure if that would weaken the power of the confession. Better to leave it.

There would be some scandal, but he knew he could rely on his uncle Walter to keep that to the minimum. And Maud would die on the rack before she confessed.

He wrote his signature, more clearly than he usually did. There must be no room for doubt. Then he took the album out of the black satchel where he'd stowed it and went over to the fire, which was crackling merrily by now. He placed the book in the middle of the flames. The leather curled immediately and the paper was devoured by the fire. He watched for a moment or two to be certain it was completely destroyed. The chime sounded in his watch and he was startled. It seemed as if another fifteen minutes had slipped out of his mind. The album was bits of ash and he was soaked with perspiration from the heat of the fire. He went over to the washstand, lifted the pitcher, and poured some water into the bowl, splashing it liberally over his face and neck. He wondered if he should shave. It seemed pointless to do so, but some niggling vanity made him decide to proceed. He opened up his razor, realized the water was cool in the bowl, and abandoned the notion. He didn't want to ring for hot water now.

The satchel where he kept his samples was standing open on the desk, waiting. Carefully, as if he were arranging a display for a customer, he removed one of the bottles, one of the cotton pads, and the wire cone. He considered praying to prepare himself, but his pain made his soul earthbound. He undressed and lay on the bed, the letter to one side, the chloroform within reach on the other. He thought about Maud and he found some peace.

CHAPTER TWENTY-SIX

"MR. PEDLOW! MR. PEDLOW! IT'S DETECTIVE MURDOCH here."

The manager of the Avonmore hovered nervously behind Murdoch and Crabtree, torn between fear and anger. Huge constables and bellowing detectives in the corridor were not conducive to good business. Already a couple of doors had opened and the curious occupants were peeking out.

"Open the door," said Murdoch to him.

Mr. Tomkin did not waste time protesting. He picked out the key from the ring and unlocked the door.

"Oh my God," he whispered and collapsed against the wall as if his legs wouldn't hold him. Murdoch, with Crabtree behind him, entered the room. The air was unpleasantly warm and thick with a sharp, stinging smell. The naked body of Henry Pedlow was lying on the bed. A cotton cloth covered his face and on top of it was a cone-shaped mask. There was a small bottle by his right hand, and a sheet of paper beneath his left. His body was in a position of repose.

"Crabtree, open all the windows, fast as you can."

Murdoch went to the body and pulled off the cloth. Leaning down, he placed his ear against the man's chest but it was a perfunctory gesture. Pedlow's heart had ceased to beat some time before.

Murdoch pulled the piece of paper from underneath the greying hand.

"To Whom It May Concern."

He could hear the hotel manager making retching noises from outside the door, and he tried not to breathe too deeply himself. Already his stomach was feeling queasy.

Crabtree joined Murdoch at the bedside, and as he saw the body he shuddered in revulsion. "Dear Lord, what was wrong with the man?"

Henry's entire torso was covered with oozing sores.

"I've seen drawings," Murdoch replied. "I'd say he had syphilis."

Crabtree shook his head in disbelief.

"Is that why he killed himself?"

"Let's see what he wrote."

Murdoch read the letter out loud to the constable, who whistled through his teeth softly when he had finished.

"So that's the story, is it? He's the one who done in the old woman."

"That's what he says."

Crabtree looked at him curiously.

Murdoch put the paper on the desk and went over to the fire, which had burned down to glowing coals. He could see the charred remnants of a leather binding, the letters... *iends*. Dolly's book of reckoning with all its shameful secrets, gone forever. Not that it mattered to him. The children were the ones who suffered most, as far as he was concerned. The innocent paid the bill of the guilty.

He glanced over his shoulder at Henry's hideous body. Was Sarah the natural child of Maud and Henry Pedlow? If that was the case and it became known, she would have no future at all. And if Walter Pedlow found out, Murdoch was certain, she would have no money even to buy a future.

"Sir? Mr. Murdoch? Shall I have Mr. Tomkin go fetch the coroner and the ambulance?" Crabtree regarded him. "The man was under sentence of death anyway by the looks of it. He's cheated the gallows is all. And a full confession helps us. He wouldn't tell a lie on his deathbed."

Murdoch picked up the poker and stirred the embers in the hearth. A last shred of the album caught fire and melted into ashes.

"You're right about that, Crabtree. Nobody will doubt it."

EPILOGUE

THE KITCHENS AND MRS. JONES AND ALWYN HAD COME out to see the games. They were seated on benches at the edge of the tug-of-war strip and were watching the police team hammer in the wooden blocks they used as wedges for the pull. There had been a thunderstorm earlier that morning and the ground was soft and muddy. Not good conditions for a tug-of-war.

"Crabtree seems fit now, Will."

Murdoch grinned at Arthur Kitchen. "He's much looser, that's why."

"Mr. Murdoch, shame on you," said Beatrice, but they all laughed. He'd told them what had happened. Brackenreid had been reluctant to abandon his poisoning theory but Crabtree had improved so dramatically when he stopped the strengthening pills that the inspector had been forced to concede.

"Watch me, Mamma," called Alwyn.

Enid Jones turned to smile at her son. He had picked up a rock and was heaving it the way he'd seen Crabtree heave the shot-put not too long ago. Murdoch was glad to see him behaving more like a healthy lad instead of the sober-eyed, clinging boy he was usually. Although he knew he was not being fair, Murdoch had felt impatient with Alwyn since the Shaw case. Lily's life had been tragic and it would be a long time before the memory of Freddie's terror and misery stopped haunting him. Thank God, Annie Brogan was doing everything she could to make up for lost time.

Alwyn ran over to his mother for a kiss and stayed there, leaning against her knees.

It was Beatrice Kitchen who'd persuaded the widow to accompany them to the tournament and Murdoch was delighted. He'd never seen Enid so carefree or so pretty. She was wearing a dress of pale pink muslin with delicate flowers on the skirt. Her white straw boater was trimmed with a green band. He thought she looked entrancing.

Henry Pedlow's death had created no stir at all in Toronto society. Murdoch heard from Louise Kenny that the story given out was that Henry had died from an accidental dose of morphine. Even his disease was described as "tropical". The coroner, of course, had ruled otherwise, but Walter seemed to have kept the newspapers away, and the verdict was never published. There was gossip in Dolly's neighbourhood for a while, but it seemed to Murdoch only two people knew the truth, himself and Maud Pedlow.

"My, you are in a study," said a merry voice from behind his shoulder.

Murdoch turned. He scrambled to his feet, tipping his straw hat. "Miss Kirkpatrick, how nice to see you."

"I wouldn't have missed it for the world. I came down with my friend and we've been wandering around ever since the race trying to find you so we could offer our congratulations."

Murdoch hadn't won, beaten by half a wheel by some wiry, bandy-legged detective from headquarters. However, he'd ridden well and he was satisfied.

"Thank you. If I had known you were watching, I would have tried even harder." He glanced around. "Where is your friend?"

"Oh, she saw someone she knew."

The Kitchens and Mrs. Jones were eyeing the young woman with frank curiosity and Murdoch hurriedly introduced them.

"Miss Kirkpatrick is in my dancing class," he said.

"And he's the best partner I've ever had," Clarice said with a laugh.

"I'm not surprised. Many a night I've heard him practising," interjected Enid. "Mind you, then, I'm not complaining. He is one of the most considerate fellow boarders imaginable."

She seemed a little flushed, and it was the most Murdoch had ever heard her say of a personal nature.

"Why, thank –"

"Men, are you ready?" called the referee, and their attention was diverted to the competition.

The twelve men on each team gave one final spit on their hands and kicked at the wooden blocks to make sure they were solidly in the ground. The thick rope lay across their feet. Crabtree was the anchor for the police team and he had wrapped the rope through the steel rings on his special leather belt.

"Oh my, you must explain the rules to me, Will," said Clarice.

"Man the rope!" shouted the referee.

Both teams picked up the heavy manila rope, holding it tight but not pulling yet. Standing to the side were the coaches. The police team's was Archie Wilson from the mounted division in number-seven station. He was a slim fellow, dressed in his best suit and hat for the occasion, and he was regarding the opponents the way he studied the horses at a sale. Get a sense who was strong, who had some weakness. Puller number four looked to be in pain. He was favouring his right leg. Use that at the crucial moment.

"Take the strain!"

With one sharp movement, all the men leaned backward, their muscles taut. The spectators who lined the strip were silent, expectant.

"Steady – pull!" The referee drove his red-and-white striped stake into the ground at the point of the white centre marker. Immediately, the grenadiers took the advantage and the red ribbon wrapped around the police team's rope moved forward two inches. Dangerous. Wilson called out.

"Hold." His voice was clear and commanding. Murdoch almost expected him to click his tongue. His men grunted. They were all wearing black knee-length drawers and sleeveless undershirts. The muscles in their calves and arms bulged. Crabtree crouched low to the ground. The team held. The ribbons didn't budge on either side.

"Yeah! Come on, George, pull." Murdoch cupped his hands and yelled at his constable.

"This is so exciting," burbled Clarice. He glanced down at her. She hardly reached to the middle of his chest if you discounted the foliage on her hat. Her face was aglow with pleasure.

"Mr. Murdoch," said Enid on his right, "what is the significance of the red ribbons?"

"They are the markers for each side. If it passes the referee's pole, the team has lost the pull."

Wilson was standing with his back to his team. His hand was behind him and he was giving signals with his fingers. Number four of the grenadiers was ready to crumble. Wilson swirled around with a little jump like a dancer.

"Now!"

The police team heaved, all together, one body. The grenadiers were dragged forward. Their marker was only three inches from the referee's pole.

"Oh, Will. I don't think I can watch." Clarice turned her head away so she was practically hiding in his arm.

"Mr. Murdoch, what are those blue bands for?" Enid touched his other sleeve.

"Pull!" cried Wilson.

"Dig!" countered the other coach.

The men dug in, grunting with the effort and took the strain. Murdoch fastened on the white marker as it wavered in the centre of the rope.

"Pull!"

It moved an inch to one side, toward the police team.

"Mr. Murdoch?" repeated Enid.

The marker moved back an inch toward the grenadiers.

Murdoch willed himself to focus his attention on the competition.

ABOUT THE AUTHOR

MAUREEN JENNINGS WAS BORN IN BIRMINGHAM,
England and emigrated to Canada at the age of seventeen.
Jennings's first novel in the Detective Murdoch series, *Except
the Dying*, was published to rave reviews and shortlisted for
both the Arthur Ellis and the Anthony first novel awards. The
influential Drood Review picked *Poor Tom Is Cold* as one of its
favourite mysteries of 2001. *Let Loose the Dogs* was shortlisted
for the 2004 Anthony Award for best historical mystery. *Night's
Child* was shortlisted for the Arthur Ellis Award, the Bruce
Alexander Historical Mystery Award, the Barry Award, and
the Macavity Historical Mystery Award. And *A Journeyman to
Grief* was nominated for the Arthur Ellis Award. Three of the

Detective Murdoch novels have been adapted for television, and a Granada International television series, *The Murdoch Mysteries*, based on the characters from the novels, is entering its fifth season on CityTV and Alibi. She lives in Toronto, Canada, with her husband Iden Ford.

Let Loose the Dogs

Detective Murdoch's life and work become tragically entwined when his sister, who long ago fled to a convent to escape their abusive father, is on her deathbed. Meanwhile, the same father has been charged with murder and calls on his estranged son to prove his innocence. But, knowing his father as he does, what is Murdoch to believe?

AVAILABLE APRIL 2012

Night's Child

After thirteen-year-old Agnes Fisher faints at school, her teacher is shocked to discover in the girl's desk two stereoscopic photographs. One is of a dead baby in its cradle and the other is of Agnes in a lewd pose. When Agnes fails to attend school the next day, her teacher takes the photographs to the police. Murdoch, furious at the sexual exploitation of such a young girl, resolves to find the photographer – and to put him behind bars.

AVAILABLE MAY 2012

Vices of My Blood

The Reverend Charles Howard sat in judgment on the poor, assessing their applications for the workhouse. But now he is dead, stabbed and brutally beaten in his office. Has some poor beggar he turned down taken his vengeance? Murdoch's investigation takes him into the world of the destitute who had nowhere else to turn when they knocked on the Reverend Howard's door.

AVAILABLE JUNE 2012

A Journeyman to Grief

In 1858, a young woman on her honeymoon is abducted, taken across the border to the US and sold into slavery. Thirty-eight years later, the owner of one of Toronto's livery stables has been found dead, horsewhipped and hung from his wrists in his tack room. The investigation endangers Murdoch's own life – and reveals how harms committed in the past can erupt fatally in the present.

AVAILABLE JULY 2012

TITANBOOKS.COM

The Harry Houdini Mysteries

BY DANIEL STASHOWER

The Dime Museum Murders
The Floating Lady Murder
The Houdini Specter (June 2012)

In turn-of-the-century New York, the Great Houdini's confidence in his own abilities is matched only by the indifference of the paying public. Now the young performer has the opportunity to make a name for himself by attempting the most amazing feats of his fledgling career—solving what seem to be impenetrable crimes. With the reluctant help of his brother Dash, Houdini must unravel murders, debunk frauds and escape from danger that is no illusion…

The Seventh Bullet
BY DANIEL D. VICTOR

The Whitechapel Horrors
BY EDWARD B. HANNA

Dr. Jekyll and Mr. Holmes
BY LOREN D. ESTLEMAN

The Angel of the Opera
BY SAM SICILIANO

The Giant Rat of Sumatra
BY RICHARD L. BOYER

The Peerless Peer
BY PHILIP JOSÉ FARMER

The Star of India
BY CAROLE BUGGÉ

COMING SOON
Titanic Tragedy
BY WILLIAM SEIL

TITANBOOKS.COM